TOMES AND THE TANGLED TRAIL

A WILLIAMS WITCH MYSTERY
BOOK TWO

ELOISE EVERHART

PB ISBN: 978-1-962759-01-4

Author: Eloise Everhart

Editors: Alyssa Hall and Kelly Reed

Cover design by GetCovers

CHAPTER 1

Charlie darted ahead of me on the sidewalk, the kitten's white tail swaying behind as he scampered back and forth. He pounced on a pebble in the walkway, only to bat it away and scurry after it, pulling against his leash. I couldn't believe that only four months ago, he could fit in the palm of my hand. Now, he was pushing nine pounds and growing quickly. I chuckled as I readjusted the box under my arm. A few more pounds, and tugs like that could pull me off balance. He was doing much better on the leash, but sometimes, his exuberance got the better of him.

We stopped outside my office building. I stared up at the red-brick facade with frosted glass windows. The window to the left said Pleasant View Insurance Agency in white letters, while the window on the right said "Williams Insurance Adjusting." I grinned as I read the signs. The frosted-glass display was the last thing to be installed during the recent remodel. My gran had owned the building and left it to me when she passed away. Originally, I only planned to come to Point Pleasant to deal with her estate, but when I arrived, it instantly felt like home. As someone who was recently divorced and unemployed, I had nothing to go back to in

Spokane. After only two weeks in town, I had decided to stay and build a life here.

I pushed through the doors and turned right, into my new office, and paused in the doorway. Charlie must have been able to sense how momentous this was because he stopped beside me and sat primly at the threshold as my gaze bounced from corner to corner. Everything was perfect.

I'd replaced the old curling vinyl with cherry hardwood floors and the stark white walls with cream paint. The warmth of the wood gave the space an inviting aura. I stepped inside and ran my fingers along an antique desk that took up the center of the room. It was a massive piece that had taken four burly men to get it into place. I'd won it at a local estate-sale auction. When I first saw the clawfoot desk, with the intricate panels and hidden compartments, it reminded me of my late friend Jessica, and I had to have it.

I set the box down and let Charlie off his leash. He swiveled his head back and forth before zooming around the room. His feet took him from one corner to another and back again in a matter of seconds. He hurled himself off the windowsill and shimmied his way under the desk, exploring every inch of his new space. I chuckled and unpacked the box, which was filled with items to personalize the space: a family photo, my favorite mug, a daily flip calendar filled with art from local artists, and a few black-and-white photos I'd taken of local landmarks and framed over the past few months. I hung them on the wall in a fun pattern.

After sprucing the space up, I moved on to the boxes left by the moving company. They'd stacked all the office equipment in the break room, where it sat waiting for me to set it up. I fidgeted with the instruction manuals as I worked. Satisfied, I stepped back to survey my work. While everything was new, the individual touches gave the room a more lived-in feel. It felt like an office someone had been coming to every day for years.

My daughter was off studying at Gonzaga University. Her fall break was one week away, and she was coming to visit Point Pleasant and my new home for the first time. Butterflies fluttered in my stomach. In one week, I would get to know if she approved of my new life. *I hope Grace loves it as much as I do.*

One more week, and I won't have much alone time. That will take some getting used to again. I chewed on the inside of my lip and stared at my purse sitting on the edge of the desk. The corner of my gran's journal peeked out at me.

The past few months hadn't been just about building a new business. I'd also been coming to terms with a secret my gran had kept from me my whole life.

We were witches.

She'd suppressed my powers most of my life, but since she was gone, they were returning. She'd left me a notebook with beginner lessons. I sighed and grabbed the notebook. The day was young, and I had a lot of things to commit to memory to fully understand my heritage. If I didn't learn it, all that knowledge would've died with my gran.

I flipped through the pages, my eyes skimming over the words as I quizzed myself. Even after four months of study, I couldn't remember it all. I could perform a handful of spells without the book, but the rest almost felt like it refused to be remembered. I stopped at the last page. My fingers hovered over the letters "1 of 7."

For weeks, I'd searched for other notebooks all through her house and office, but I hadn't found a single one of them yet. My gran's friend, Betty, knew something, but she refused to speak. She kept giving me a knowing smile and told me over and over, "When you're ready..." I traced the numbers with my fingertips. I'd touched them so many times that the only emotion I could pick up—using an ability Betty told me was called psychometry—was my own. The emotion on that page only read as frustration.

3

As the door to my office swung open, I jumped in my seat and dropped the book.

"Knock, knock." Olivia said, poking her head inside. She worked across the hall at the agency. Since having her baby, she'd switched to a more relaxed but still fashionable look. She wore a yellow-and-red wrap dress over knee-length boots and had her curly black hair up in a high puff.

Heather also popped her head in around the corner. Her red hair had gotten longer over the past few months, and she wore it braided in a circlet around her head. "Good morning, Dani. Is it okay if we come in?"

"Of course!" I crouched, grabbed the book, and tucked it back into my purse. "What are you guys doing here so early?"

"Liv texted me yesterday, saying the last of the work trucks had gone." Heather let out a low whistle as she walked around the space. "You didn't think we would miss celebrating this momentous occasion with you? You're opening your doors today for the first time. That's huge! And this space looks amazing."

Olivia followed her into the room, her hands held behind her back. "And what type of neighbor would I be if I didn't formally welcome you to the building?"

They were one of the big reasons I'd stayed. After the divorce, I'd felt cut off from my prior life and was floating along, adrift. They both threw me a life buoy and made me feel like I belonged.

I blinked back a tear. "Oh, you guys. Thank you!"

"I got you something." Olivia pulled a box out from behind her back and shoved it toward me.

I took the nondescript box from her and turned it over. I quirked an eyebrow at her as I pried it open. She grinned. Inside was a gray hoodie. I pulled it out. The fabric was soft and medium weight—perfect for Whidbey Island winters. I flipped it over and froze, a wide smile spreading across my face. On the back was my company's logo and name. She'd made me a hoodie that I could wear out on the job. It was perfect.

Olivia squealed. "Charlie!"

Heather crouched to pet him when he poked his head out from under my desk. "He's so big! At this rate, he's going to be bigger than his mother."

Olivia reached into her bag. "I may have gotten him a welcome-to-the-building gift as well."

"Oh, really?" I asked.

"Our shared office space could really use a mascot." She unwrapped and held up a kerchief with a checkered pattern.

The plaid alternated between gray and red. On the gray squares was my office logo, and on the red squares was the logo for the agency across the hall. I grinned and nodded.

She crouched down next to Charlie and tied it around his neck. "What do you think?"

Charlie strutted away. He turned his head and peered at me over his shoulder then pranced back toward us, his tail held high.

"Very dashing." I clapped.

Heather stood and smoothed her shirt. "I have some news too. Yesterday, I successfully found a home for the last of Star's other kittens. And just in time too. The local vet called me not five minutes later. Someone left a box of kittens at his door, and he thought of me."

"How are they doing?" I asked.

Heather smiled. "Great. They are old enough they don't need to be bottle-fed, which is good. I have them set up in my apartment in what I have dubbed the kitten room. Star has taken to them. She was so attentive to their needs last night. It was adorable."

Olivia readjusted the kerchief around Charlie's neck one last time and stood. "Are you still looking for a home for Star?"

"No." Heather beamed. "The cat cafe is really becoming

something, and all kittens need a good foster mom. She's here to stay."

My phone dinged in my purse. I grabbed it but saw no notifications. The dinging sound came again, from deeper in my purse. My hands trembled as I rummaged for another cell phone, which I'd bought for work. Its screen lit up as I pulled it out. My breath caught in my throat. I'd received a new email. I opened it up and read the title: "New Assignment."

"Oh my gosh. I've received my first claim."

The email was from an old co-worker. I had hoped and dreamed that I would get a claim on my first day, but seeing it as a reality was more than I'd expected. My whole body felt lighter, and I bounced in place as a grin spread across my face. "I have work to do."

Olivia and Heather surged forward and pulled me into a three-way hug. "Congratulations," they said almost simultaneously.

I stifled a giggle as they released me.

Heather squeezed my shoulder. "Promise to stop by the cafe later to tell me how it goes?"

"I promise."

They congratulated me a few more times before gathering their things and leaving my office. I was still grinning when I powered on my computer for the first time. This was my first claim as an independent adjuster. My new life was really beginning.

Once I got into the system, I pulled the email up and read through the documents my former coworker had sent over with it. He said it was a test case, and if it went well, he would send me more work. *No pressure.* I chewed on my lip. "Fire damage to rental property. Possible total loss," the file said. I'd half hoped my first claim, especially a test-case claim, would be something simple so that I could start out on the right foot. This sounded like the damage was going to be extensive, which meant it was complicated. *I can handle complicated claims. I won't start doubting myself now. I've been doing this for eighteen years.* I shook my head and got to work setting up the file.

After the administrative work was done, I sat staring at my work phone. I'd made thousands of phone calls as a claims adjuster, but this was the first one where I was my own boss. I would have a lot of firsts today.

I dialed the property manager, who answered on the second ring. "Hi, is this Carol? My name's Dani, with Williams Adjusting. I'm the adjuster assigned to assist you with the fire damage claim on Vanguard."

Keys clacked in the background. "I don't have a lot of information on it. We were called by the fire department last night. From what I understand, the fire investigator is still on site."

"Okay. I'll swing by to see if they've released the home. I see on the loss notice that there is a tenant in the home, a Miss Tina Monroe. Do you have her phone number?"

"Yeah." A dog whined in the background. She shushed it and whispered something about going on a walk in a minute. "We haven't heard from her yet. I hope she found someplace safe to stay."

We chatted for a few more minutes. The property manager really didn't have a lot of information. The fire had only been out for a few hours. I probably wouldn't be able to inspect it that day, but it didn't hurt to check it out. Charlie had fallen asleep in a sunspot on the window ledge while I worked. I scratched him behind his ears, and he curled up into a tighter ball. I left him there, threw on my new hoodie, and headed out to meet the local fire inspector.

CHAPTER 2

The scent of smoke hung heavy in the air. It hit me for the first time when I was over two blocks away and grew stronger the closer I got to the home. The smell was at odds with the quiet neighborhood. All the homes were in the Craftsman style popular in the 1920s. While older, everything was well maintained. The lawns were all manicured. Trees lined the streets. Almost every other house had the iconic white picket fence enclosing the front yard, but the scent of burned wood gave the neighborhood a foreboding atmosphere.

I parked across the street from the house, behind the fire investigator's white Ford pickup. The house almost appeared to have been cut in half. The front was completely gone. The only thing that remained was the scorched foundation and one wooden support beam that had burned and snapped. It hung over the empty lot, threatening to break off at any minute. The rear of the house was somewhat intact. From the street, I could see blackened kitchen cabinets and half a staircase leading to nothing.

I tore my gaze away from the home to take in the surroundings. The houses in the neighborhood had been built about twenty feet apart. While they weren't cramped at that distance, I would've expected to see more damage to the house next door. It had a singed fence and a light dusting of soot on its siding but didn't appear to have suffered any structural damage. I scanned the area. The streets were empty but with signs of recent activity. Deep grooves stood out in the frozen earth of the front yard, where the fire trucks had driven up onto the sidewalk. Across the street were irregular patches of disturbed frost, where people had huddled together to watch the blaze. I jotted down a few notes before getting out of my car.

I opened my trunk, peered into my home-inspection kit, and settled for grabbing a pair of boot covers and my camera. The city probably wanted to get that beam down before they let anyone inside.

I ambled toward the house, snapping a few pictures as I went. I paused in the front yard and squinted into the wreckage. It was far enough away that I couldn't make out too many details, but in the middle of what had probably been the living room was a pile of burned-out tires. The tires were warped and deflated, the black turned to gray. I scrunched up my nose at their distinctive odor. Under the wood smoke was the caustic scent of burned rubber. I raised my camera, zoomed in, and snapped a photo.

I studied the damage through the lens. Around the tire, everything was either melted or so severely scorched that I couldn't tell what things were. Farther away from the tire, some things held their shape. I snapped a few more pictures. Determining the origin was going to be easy, but that begged the questions "Why were there tires in the living room?" and "Who set them on fire?" *Tina?*

I continued walking around the structure, taking a few more quick photos as I looked for the investigator. I rounded the house to the backyard. Standing at the back door was a man wearing work boots, jeans, and a reflective jacket over a white button-up shirt. He held a helmet under his left arm and a clipboard in his right hand. His broad shoulders slumped forward as he wrote.

I cleared my throat and strode forward, a hand raised in greeting. "Good morning. Are you the fire investigator?"

He scowled. As his eyes settled on my face, his expression shifted to a smile. "I am. Brad Parsons. And you are?"

"Dani Williams, with Williams Insurance Adjusting." I pulled out a business card and handed it to him as he came down the back stairs.

He shoved it into one of his pockets without reading it. "And what can I help you with today, ma'am?" he asked, his Southern drawl becoming more pronounced on the word *ma'am*.

I smiled at him. "The property owner's insurance company has hired me to inspect the damages. Do you know when the home is going to be released?"

He scratched at his head and glanced back into the home. "We just finished checking it out for hot spots. I want to give it another day to settle and get that beam down. It should be available tomorrow."

"Excellent. If anything changes, will you let me know?" I shielded my eyes and peered up at him through my fingers.

"Sure thing."

I left him to continue his work and retreated to my car. A day's wait wasn't too bad. I started making a mental to-do list as I packed away my camera. As I closed the trunk, the hair on the back of my neck stood up. *Someone's watching me.* My head jerked up, and I whirled around.

The street was empty.

After what had happened with Marsha, I had been a little jumpier. Something about having a killer's hands wrapped around my throat had left me on high alert, even months later. I rubbed a hand against my pant leg and slowly swiveled in place, my eyes darting from window to window, searching for the watcher.

A curtain twitched in a window of the house I'd parked in front of. I swallowed and closed my eyes. *Just because they were watching doesn't mean they were up to no good.* I'd inherited powers from my gran that she called the Sight. I'd always had good intuition, but since she passed and my powers had developed, my intuition was becoming more powerful. It rarely guided me wrong. I cleared my thoughts and slowed my breathing, letting my mind settle.

Once the initial shock of discovering someone was watching me wore off, I whispered to myself, "What do they want? Why were they watching me?" and waited for my intuition to kick in.

It didn't take long. Curiosity. Concern. Their gaze hadn't contained anything malicious. *A witness?* I smiled and opened my eyes. I stared up at the house. The curtain twitched again, and I made eye contact with a scrawny man with disheveled blond hair. He blinked, and the curtain closed again.

I walked up the sidewalk to his house and knocked. It was quiet. I knocked again, more loudly that time. Feet shuffled inside, and a chain rattled. The door popped open a few inches, and the man from the window peeked out at me. He'd smoothed his hair into place and thrown a black robe on over his red plaid pajamas.

"Yes?" His voice was at odds with his body. It was deep, and the sound reverberated in the small covered entryway.

I fished a business card out of my pocket. "Good morning. Sorry to bother you so early, but I was hoping you might be able to help me with something."

He blinked, looking between the outstretched card and my face. He didn't take it. I shoved it back into my pocket and smiled. "I'm investigating the fire across the way. Were you home last night?"

He nodded.

"Excellent. I know the fire was pretty late. Did it wake you up at all?"

He shook his head.

"Oh, man. I was hoping you might have seen something. Did you sleep through it, then?" I fought the urge to fidget. My instincts were screaming at me, telling me he knew something—hard to tell if the feeling came from my magic or all the years on the job or both. As an adjuster, I developed the sense of when someone was holding something back. He had that deer-caught-in-headlights look on his face. If I pushed too hard, he would close the door, and I wouldn't find anything out.

"No," he croaked. "I was up."

"Did you know Tina?" I asked.

His face softened. "Not well. She reminded me of my daughter." He pulled the door open the rest of the way. "Normally, I work swing shifts, but it was my night off. I hate sleeping right when I get off work, so I usually stay up late to unwind. Last night, I was watching Netflix when I noticed the fire. I ran out barefoot in my pajamas and grabbed a hose from the side of my house. The fire was going pretty good at that point, my hose didn't do much, so I started spraying the neighboring properties down. I thought maybe, you know, if they were wet, they wouldn't catch too."

"That's pretty quick thinking. You might have saved their houses. How long did it take for the fire department to arrive?"

He pursed his lips, thinking. "Five minutes, maybe? They were on the scene pretty quick. I had barely made it outside when I first heard their sirens in the distance."

"Now, we always have to ask—do you remember seeing anything or anyone strange in the area before the fire started?"

He swallowed and peered behind me. I followed his eyes to a tree overhanging Tina's side gate.

"Did you see someone at the gate?" I asked.

"At least an hour before the fire, though. I realized I had forgotten to take my trash in from the curb, you know? So I went out to grab it around eleven o'clock. It was dark out already, but I saw someone walking out the back door. They ducked under that tree and walked a block to their car. I thought it was strange because there's always available street parking in this neighborhood. Why park so far away?"

"Did you get a good look at them?"

"No. It was too dark to see them clearly."

"Did you see what type of car they were driving?"

"A red Ford Explorer."

"Could it have been Tina?"

He squeezed his eyes closed, and his voice cracked as he answered. "They pulled that poor girl out this morning. Loaded her into the coroner's van. I didn't realize she was in there. I should have thought about it, you know? Maybe if I had gone inside…"

I patted him on his shoulder. He slumped and curled in on himself, becoming smaller. We stood there in silence, my mind reeling. I would have to tell the insurance company. I bit my lip. Fatalities had a way of making claims much more complicated. *It's a test case. Will they still trust me with it? Would they transfer the case to someone else?* If I wanted to keep the file, I needed to bring them something useful when I reported the news to prove to them I could handle it.

"Is there anything else you need?" he mumbled.

"No." I took a step back. "Thank you so much for your time. And… my condolences."

He backed away into his house, closing the door. I stared at the tree next to the burnt house. I scanned the street. No one else was watching. I squared my shoulders, darted across the roadway, and stopped under the tree. The branches were a few inches over my head. I put one fist on top of my head then the other. I had small hands, and when clenched into fists, they were exactly three inches across. My second fist brushed up against the tree limb. Whoever ducked under the tree was at least half a foot taller than me, so they had to be six feet tall at a minimum.

I lowered my arms. The roadway was clear. At half past eight in the morning, almost all the daily commuters were on the road. I peered up at the tree, studying the branches. Halfway across that lowest branch was a twig that jutted down at an awkward angle. It was almost snapped in two—the only thing keeping it together was a piece of bark. By the looks of it, the twig had probably hung down directly in the walking path, and the break was recent. The wood was raw and showed no signs of wear. Hesitantly, I raised my fingers and brushed them against the wood.

My eyes widened, and a muscle twitched in my neck. My heart raced, and my fists involuntarily clenched. The emotion coming off the twig was hard to place, a mix of rage and desperation. I flinched back from the twig and rubbed my hand against my jeans.

The hair on the back of my neck stood up again. My head snapped down. Frozen in the backyard, only ten feet away, was Brad, the fire investigator. He raised his hand in an awkward wave. I smiled and waved back.

"You forget something?" he asked.

I shook my head. "Just checking the tree for fire damage. It's a beauty."

I hurried back to my car. He stood watching me for a few more seconds before returning to the house. I exhaled and hung my head. *Way to look like a weirdo on my very first claim. I need to focus.* I started the engine. My hands hovered over the steering wheel. *That was a powerful emotion, and this fire looks an awful lot like arson. Tires take a lot of work to light, but once they're going, they are twice as difficult to put back out. What if she was murdered?* I shook myself.

The sheriff didn't appreciate me sticking my nose in

where it didn't belong, but my poking around was the only reason Jessica's killer had been brought to justice. *I have to investigate the claim. Tina's death just happens to be part of it, right? What harm will it do to check in on the medical examiner? If they found the tenant dead in the house, I have to rule out a liability claim anyway. This isn't because I don't trust the sheriff to get things done.*

I pulled away from the curb and drove. *A few questions won't hurt anyone.*

The medical examiner's office was tucked away in a residential neighborhood, in what used to be a funeral home. From the street, the old, rambling Victorian looked similar to the other houses on the block. The only things that truly gave it away were the nondescript sign in the front yard and the extra pipe chimneys poking out of the roof in the back. They had a distinctive look, though the crematorium wasn't in use anymore.

I let myself into the foyer. The sounds from the street disappeared as the door shut behind me. The building was only slightly warmer inside than out. Victor Shaw, the medical examiner, kept it chilly year round. I rubbed my hands together for warmth as I looked around.

The last time I'd been inside was after my gran died. Victor did his best to soften the blow, but nobody can make grief comfortable. It hollows you out, stripping away every ounce of happiness until only the hole remains—for a time, at least. I let out a shaky breath. Being there brought that feeling back. The hole in my heart where Gran had been remained empty. But joy had come back into my life, filling in around the edges. The hole continued to sting but had become bearable.

The place had changed little since then. Everything was

some variation of beige. The ceramic tile floor was made of overlapping white circles in a sea of tan. Faded wooden beams led upstairs. Cream curtains hung over the windows, letting in thin, diffused light. My gran used to joke when I was a child that in the dictionary under the entry "silly" was a picture of me. A picture of this room would be under the word "bland."

I stepped up to the counter and pushed the buzzer. A bell rang deep in the house, a punctuated, deep sound almost like a church bell ringing in a Gothic cathedral. While the decorations in the entryway were bland, Victor was the opposite. He shuffled into view, wearing the classic doctor's coat over a Regency-style men's suit. His white hair was styled in a neat pompadour, with a thick, tidy beard covering the bottom half of his face. He smiled when he saw me, his bright-blue eyes twinkling.

"Victor! Are you alone here today?"

"Afraid so. I had heard you were staying in town. What brings you in?" He pulled me into a quick hug. When I breathed him in, he smelled of sandalwood and thyme. Victor had been there when both my grandpa and my gran had passed. He had a comforting presence, very fatherly. I could imagine him wrapping me up in a blanket and shoving hot cocoa into my hands.

I hugged him and stepped back. "I'm working on a claim for the house fire. From what I heard, the tenant passed away, and I wanted to see if I could get a timeline on things. Do you know when the death certificate will be available?"

He frowned. "I'll need the next of kin's permission to release it to you."

"I was planning on working on that later today."

He nodded, still frowning. "You have plenty of time. The autopsy is ongoing."

"Really?" I half choked on my words, hoping I was wrong,

but my instincts were rarely wrong. "Didn't she die in the fire?"

He chewed on his lip, his eyes flicking behind me.

"I can't help but think how close in age she is to my daughter, Grace, you know?" I reached forward and touched his arm, holding his gaze.

He exhaled sharply and leaned in toward me. He whispered in a conspiratorial tone. "It's too early to tell right now for sure. I need to do a full workup. But right now? I am treating this as a homicide."

My eyes widened. "A homicide?"

He nodded. "No smoke in the lungs. It'll be at least two weeks before I have a more formalized report."

I left his office in a daze. At the scene, I'd suspected something bad had happened, but having it confirmed rattled me. I climbed into my car and stared blankly ahead. *This is such a sleepy town. Two murders in less than a year?* That was almost unbelievable. But I'd felt the rage on the broken branch. The burned tire was unmistakable.

Someone had murdered Tina Monroe.

CHAPTER 3

I drove straight to the Bizzy Bean, Heather's cafe. Heather had commissioned a wonderful window display artist out of Port Angeles. They came by monthly to update the artwork. It had become a shop tradition, that they would close for the afternoon on the first Sunday of every month and cover the windows. The regulars would gather outside, with bated breath, to see the new design. It coincided with Heather launching the monthly cupcake special. Since she had started the conversion into a cat cafe, the artwork in the windows had shifted from her classic bees-and-flower theme to cats trying to play with bees.

This month's display was especially adorable. Taking up almost the entire window was a painting of a large white cat sitting primly with a bee at the end of her nose—her bright-blue eyes were crossed as she stared at it. It was a rendition of Heather's rescue cat. The artist had perfectly captured the star pattern on her chest and the caramel swirl that ended in a tip between her eyes. I smiled, staring at the glass painting in the window, and the stress from the day receded.

Star, the inspiration for the window display, greeted me at the door. She threw herself into my legs, rubbing against them and purring up a storm. After she greeted me, she looked around my legs for Charlie. When she didn't find him, she looked up at me quizzically.

I kneeled to pet her, but she backed out of reach. "Sorry, Star. He isn't with me today."

She swished her tail, raised her head, sticking her nose straight up in the air, and sauntered off.

"Well, it's good to see you too." I chuckled.

I stood and surveyed the cafe. I'd spent the past few months dealing with my grandmother's estate and setting up a new business. My daily visits had changed to weekly and, for the past month, had dried up altogether as paperwork ate all of my free time. While I recognized the giant cat castle that took up the entire left wall, I didn't recognize all the new art. For as long as I could remember, every inch of bare wall was covered in bee art. Over the past month, Heather had changed out the photos and paintings for a combination of bee and cat pictures. The sign over the counter had changed as well, now reading "The Bizzy Bean, a.k.a. Cafe Meow" in bold black-and-yellow print. The *o* in "Meow" was star shaped.

Heather stood under the sign, taking an order from a couple of tourists. I waved at her. When she looked over at me, I cocked my head to the back table. She nodded, and I turned, almost slamming into the Retirees.

Agnes, Betty, and Sarah gathered around me, speaking over each other.

"It's been a few days since we noticed a work truck outside your office," Agnes began.

"And the tarps came down yesterday," Betty chimed in next.

Sarah inched in closer to touch my arm. "Have you finally opened your doors?"

I chuckled. "Today was the big day."

Agnes beamed. "That's fantastic news. Have you gotten your first customer yet?"

"I have." I peeked behind me, where Heather was still working behind the counter. "I received my first claim this morning."

"Oh, that is so exciting!" Betty said.

Agnes pulled me into a hug. "By the end of the day, I'm sure you'll have more customers than you'll know what to do with."

"I don't know about that." I pulled back. "It's going to be a slow trickle until I've proven myself."

"Is that why you went with such a quiet opening?" Sarah asked.

The Retirees exchanged a glance then all began talking at once. Making out what each of them said was difficult as they crowded closer. I stepped back and bumped into the door.

"I think what we were trying to ask..." Betty swatted the other two away, glaring at them. "How is anyone supposed to know you're in business if you haven't done a grand opening?"

"I know I have an office downtown, but my customers aren't part of the general public. They're insurance companies."

I looked from Agnes to Betty to Sarah. They wore identical red track suits. I stifled a grin because they almost looked like they'd lined up by hair color on purpose. Agnes's hair was completely white, cut short into a curly bob. Betty's was almost an even split between gray and brown, her straight hair brushed against her shoulders. Sarah's was more black than white, her strips of white hair framing her face, stark against her terra-cotta skin, and trailing halfway down her back. Their eyebrows were raised. Sarah pursed her lips in thought.

"Now that I'm open for business, though, I had been

thinking about reaching out to a few of my contacts to let them know. I only told a couple of people, to start."

Agnes cocked her head to one side. "But how are you going to entice them in?"

That hit me like a ton of bricks. I didn't have a backup plan. This was it. My shoulders tensed. *That's a good question.*

"Why don't you make gift baskets?" Betty asked, placing her hand on my shoulder. She was always good at sensing the mood shift.

"I can help with that," Heather said, her approach half hidden by the Retirees crowding around me. "A little something sweet, especially around the holiday season. It'll warm them right up."

I grinned. "That sounds like a great idea."

She glanced at the Retirees crowding around me. "I'll be at the counter when you're ready to order."

"I'm ready now." I extricated myself from the circle and followed Heather.

Behind me, the group wandered back over to their usual table, and their voices carried through the room. Within seconds, their conversation had moved on to more serious issues: whether the Christmas tree at the town hall should be put up before or after Thanksgiving.

"Thanks," I whispered to Heather.

She grinned. "They mean well. But they can come across like a pack of piranhas when they get excited about something. Now, what can I get you?"

I stared blankly at the menu overhead. Since I was no longer surrounded, the stress of the day settled upon me, draining me of energy. I slumped forward. "Something with a lot of caffeine."

Heather studied me. "Everything okay? Did your first claim not go well?"

"No. Not exactly. It's complicated."

Late in the day, there were not many customers. There

was only one woman standing behind me. She was engrossed with her phone, her beach-blond waves falling forward to conceal her face. Heather looked between her and me. "Ma'am. I will be right back." She looped her arm around my shoulders and dragged me to a table in the back. I slid into the booth and sagged onto the padded bench. "Wait here." She darted back to the counter to take the woman's order.

A few minutes later, she came back with a steaming mug in one hand and Star clasped to her chest by the other. She deposited Star in my arms and set the mug in front of me. Star stared up at me for a second then turned in a circle in my lap and settled down to make biscuits on my thigh. I pet her, her purrs vibrating under my hand.

"What happened?" Heather slid into the booth across from me.

I glanced over at the Retirees, who were distracted by their Christmas tree concerns. They were permanent fixtures on various community-planning committees. Sarah was overseeing a local fundraiser for the food pantry. Thanksgiving was one of their biggest donation days. She was arguing that if the Christmas tree went up before the fundraiser, it would pull focus. I had to admit that she had a point. The Christmas display was always so vibrant and joyful. I loved it so much that it was hard not to agree with Betty that it should go up early. The town could use a boost of festivity. Especially with the tension over the mayoral race.

Heather cut into my thoughts. "That bad, huh?"

"The claim I got was for a fire." I sighed and leaned back as Star shifted on my lap and gave me a dirty look before resettling. "They found a body. And... it looks like she might have been murdered."

She gasped, covering her mouth. "What does that mean for you?"

"It probably won't change much for me. For my client,

maybe. But my job stays the same." I shifted in my seat, and Star jumped down and sauntered off. "The tenant was a college student. I can't help but think about Grace."

Heather squeezed my hand. "What does Chris have to say about it?"

I blushed. Chris, the local deputy, was a childhood friend. Until recently, I'd assumed he was friendlier to my ex-husband than to me, but we'd become a lot closer after my brush with death at the hands of Jessica's killer. "I haven't spoken to him about it."

Heather scoffed and playfully swatted at me. "Why not? Isn't one perk of dating the deputy getting the inside scoop on crime?"

My blush deepened. "We're only having coffee together."

"Weekly." She smirked. "And I have eyes. I've seen how you guys look at each other."

I cleared my throat. "We're just friends."

She rolled her eyes. "And as friends… why not ask him for the inside scoop?"

I fidgeted under her gaze and slowly sipped the rest of my coffee. I didn't have a suitable answer. After I found out, I could've texted him, but if he didn't want to talk to me about it, he might call off our coffee dates. There I was, calling it a date. *Coffee… hangouts?*

The bell above the door chimed, and a serious-looking man in a crisp black suit stepped through the door, carrying a clipboard. He squinted down at Star as she greeted him at the door, and he jotted something down.

"I should probably get this." Heather slid out of the booth and walked over, smiling.

She greeted him and shooed Star away. Her smile shifted to a straight line as they spoke. He pulled out a pair of white gloves and began walking around the space. She trailed behind him, answering his questions. He jotted a few more things down. He jabbed at the paper and thrust the cap back onto his pen before continuing with his inspection.

I slid out of the booth and wandered toward the counter. I took my time returning my cup so that I could listen in on their conversation.

"We had a health inspection three months ago."

He murmured something back to her and yanked the cap back off his pen. He wrote furiously across the page, his pen so loud that I could hear the scratches from where I stood.

"Yes, the A-plus rating was reconfirmed. Is there some sort of problem?" Heather twisted her hands in front of her.

I frowned. I hovered, debating between joining Heather or giving her space. The woman with the beach-blond hair dropped her coffee cup off behind me and went back to fiddling with her phone. Her standing behind me put my nerves on edge. I gritted my teeth. Lingering might add more stress to her life. Heather didn't need any more complications right now. I walked toward the door. Heather would have her hands full for a while. As I passed, I squeezed her shoulder.

"You've got this," I whispered before heading out the door.

Health inspections were always random. But a second one so soon after her last was odd. *I hope it isn't serious.*

Charlie was waiting back at the office for me to come pick him up. As I drove, I made a quick mental checklist. I didn't have much of an update to give my client yet but decided I should probably tell them about Tina, just in case they didn't know the claim involved a fatality. With rental properties, it sometimes took a surprisingly long time for information to filter its way to the insurance company.

CHAPTER 4

Charlie dashed into the house ahead of me and flopped down on the couch. He sprawled, stretching his limbs as far as they would go before curling up into a ball.

"Rough day, buddy?" I set my stuff down and walked into the kitchen.

He opened a single eye and watched me move around the room. When I disappeared into the kitchen, he raised his head and rested his chin on the armrest to keep me in view.

"It was for me too."

I busied myself with reheating leftovers. As I worked, I told him about my day. His eyes widened when I told him about Tina's potential murder and slow blinked at me as I described my meeting with Heather and his mother, Star. He almost seemed to understand me. *Do witches have familiars?* I mentally added that to the list of questions I had for Betty. Maybe that was a question she would actually answer. Whenever I was with Charlie, though, I felt calmer. It didn't matter if witches didn't have familiars—a genuine connection was there.

I took a seat in the breakfast nook and played with my phone while I ate. My daughter, Grace, had read my messages throughout the week but hadn't responded. I bit my lip. Over the past year, she'd been hot and cold. Some days, we still felt close, and other days, we seemed like strangers. Teenagers were always difficult. *She was fiery even before the divorce.* I pecked out a message with one finger: "Opened the doors to Williams' Adjusting for the first time today."

She read the message right away. I stared at the screen, waiting for the triple dots to appear to show she was typing. After a minute, I sent one last message: "Hope your midterms are going well. Miss you." After dropping the phone, I slid it away from me and turned my attention to my bowl of bacon-topped mac and cheese.

The house was quiet. The thin carpet in the living room did little to muffle the sound of my footsteps. *Now that the office is done, maybe I should change things up at the house too.* I sat down next to Charlie on the couch.

I pulled out my gran's journal and read through the various spells again. She'd dedicated the bulk of the book to spells that recalled the memory of an object. That was different from my innate ability to pick up emotional residue from objects. When I cast the spell, it was like I was the object. I had successfully cast the basic version several times but hadn't attempted the more complicated versions. Every time I sat down to try, my palms became sweaty, and I would suddenly remember I had something else to do. I flipped open the book and read the spell. The basic version should allow me to experience the recent memory of an object as it had experienced it. The more complicated versions would let me delve further back and included insights provided by the Sight. It was, according to the notes, half prophetic vision and half memory.

Over the past two months, I'd improved my skills. If I wanted to understand my gran's legacy and find the other books, I needed to challenge myself. I hadn't pushed myself and had stalled out in my studies. The only way forward was through. I gritted my teeth. *Fear will not dictate my life.* After rereading through the directions one last time, I got up to create a space to practice. I cleared the center of the living room and laid out a white sheet with a pentagram painted on it in black. I grabbed one of my gran's knickknacks from the shelf, a miniature Eiffel Tower she'd picked up in Europe when she was a teenager, and placed it at the tip of the pentagram farthest from me. At each of the remaining four corners, I placed objects that evoked the senses and reminded me of the place she'd purchased it.

I moved from corner to corner, placing objects. On the top left, I placed coffee beans for their smell. I placed macaroons from the bakery on the top right tip to represent the sense of taste. I played jazz music on my phone and put it on the bottom right, followed by a photo from my gran's vacation in the bottom left. After crouching in the center in front of the Eiffel Tower, I began.

It was a multistep process that required me to layer six spells on top of each other before I brought it all together by touching the tower and activating the Sight. I whispered the words of the first spell. Golden light trickled out of my mouth and floated around the coffee. I whispered the words to the second spell. More light spilled out of me and floated toward the macaroons. The two lines of light danced and merged in the center, connecting all three of us together.

A grin broke out across my face, and I whispered the words of the third spell. Light spilled from my mouth and was halfway to my cell phone when my phone rang, cutting off the music. I flinched at the sound. The light flickered and pulsed. I tried to push forward and regain control, but the phone rang a second time, and the light and the spell dissipated before they could take hold.

I sighed, picked up my phone. "Hey, honey."

"Oh, um," a woman stuttered, "is Danielle Williams available?"

I blinked. This was my personal line, so no one other than family and friends called me at that number. "Yes. This is Dani."

"My name's Izzy Carter. I'm a reporter for the *Island County Gazette.*" She paused.

Why is a reporter calling me?

"Hello? Are you still there?"

I slid to the ground, my legs splaying out to one side. "Yes. I'm here."

Izzy exhaled sharply. "Excellent. I'm writing an article on the fire on Vanguard. I understand you're the adjuster assigned to the claim."

I scrunched my eyebrows together. "I'm sorry, but how did you get this number?"

She laughed a nervous laugh. "I was hoping to ask you a few questions about the investigation. How is it coming along?"

"What?"

"The investigation? Into the fire? You are Danielle Williams, with Williams Adjusting, correct?"

The doorbell rang.

I scrambled to my feet. "I am."

"House fires like this are so uncommon on an island like this. People are worried. Does it have anything to do with the trash can fires discovered all over town for the past few months?"

Trash can fires? What is she talking about? I shuffled toward the door as someone knocked a second time. "Hold on a second. Someone's at the door."

I opened the front door. Standing on the porch, with bags around her feet, was Grace.

My jaw dropped, and I stuttered into the phone, "I'm sorry. I can't discuss the claim without my client's permission. If you have questions about the homicide investigation, I would recommend reaching out to the sheriff's office. I've got to go."

I hung up and stared at Grace as she grabbed her bags and strode into the house.

"Where's my room?" Grace paused at the mouth of the hallway.

"I wasn't expecting you until next week." My eyes flicked to my spell circle in the middle of the living room, and I kicked the corner of the sheet to flip it over. One macaroon flew off and slid under the couch. "Aren't you supposed to be taking your midterms right now?"

"I'm moving in. Is it still the second door on the left, or am I upstairs?"

"Moving in? What about school?"

Grace hunched her shoulders and gripped the handles of her bags, her knuckles turning white. "I've decided to take a gap year."

"Does your dad know where you are?" I stepped toward her, a hand raised. My fingertips hovered over her shoulder.

She shook. "If you don't want me here, I can leave."

"Oh, honey. I'll always want you here." I spun her around, pulling her into a hug. "Did something happen?"

Grace wrapped her hands around my waist and buried her head into my shoulder. "I'm just tired, Mom. I realized I didn't know what I wanted to do, and... I need a break. Is that okay?"

"Of course. Take all the time you need."

She pulled back and wiped her eyes. "Am I in the guest bedroom?" She sniffled.

I nodded and smoothed her hair back from her heart-shaped face. She had my dark-brown hair and her father's brown eyes. She averted her gaze.

"Are you okay, sweetie?"

"I'm tired." She grabbed her bags and strode away down the hall.

I stood wavering in the hallway. After a minute, I followed her to the guest bedroom. She'd dropped her bags in the doorway, kicked off her shoes, and was lying facedown on the bedspread. She was already asleep.

I stood watching her for a few minutes. *Did something happen?* I grabbed her bags from the floor, and a wave of fatigue washed over me. I put a hand out to steady myself. Breathing slowly, I refocused. I pushed the fatigue aside and unpacked the bags while she slept. Charlie soon appeared in the doorway and looked between Grace and me. He jumped up on the bed next to her and sniffed her face. They hadn't met yet.

"This is Grace, my daughter," I told him.

He blinked and sniffed at her again.

I pulled the last of her clothes out of her duffel bag and folded it up.

"Okay, let's go," I whispered.

Charlie flopped down next to her and rested his head on her shoulder.

"Buddy, let's go."

He closed his eyes.

I chuckled to myself and left her room, leaving the door open a crack in case Charlie wanted to come out later. I returned to the living room and cleaned up the spell circle. The coffee had scattered. I kneeled to pick up the few stray beans the broom had missed and fished the macaroon out from under the couch. While Grace hadn't noticed it when she came in, if it was there when she got up, she was going to ask questions. I wasn't ready for the "I'm a witch" conversation yet.

Someday.

But not today.

I retreated to my room and climbed into bed, clutching

the journal to my chest. I tossed and turned in bed as the day replayed through my head. It hadn't gone the way I'd expected. One day into my new venture as an independent claim adjuster, and I'd already stumbled into a murder investigation. *Would the reporter make things more difficult? The sheriff had barely squeaked by in his reelection bid. Would this make him take the investigation more seriously than he had Jessica's? Or would he rush things as he always does? It's out of my control. I should handle the claim like I normally do. Right? And Grace...*

I stared up at the ceiling, unable to sleep. *How am I supposed to talk to her about being a witch? Gran, why did you hide this from me for so long? I'm in the dark. How am I supposed to know if she is one or not too?* I pushed those thoughts from my head and focused on the achievements of the day. I had successfully cast the first third of the spell. I was certain I could do the whole thing correctly the next time I tried. Smiling, I rolled over and drifted off to sleep.

CHAPTER 5

Early the next morning, I shuffled through the house, packing my things and preparing for the day. I poked my head into Grace's room. She'd moved under the covers sometime in the night, but she was still fast asleep. She lay with one arm draped across her pillow, Charlie curled into a ball against her chest. Her cheek rested against his back. He opened one of his eyes when I came into the room, but when I called for him, he closed it and pretended to be sleeping.

We'd never owned pets before. Charlie was my first. They were so peaceful sleeping together. I retreated to the kitchen, where I scrawled a quick note and left it on the fridge.

Hey, honey,

I hope you slept well. Sorry there isn't a lot of food in the house yet. I'd planned to stock up before your visit, but things got away from me with the grand opening. If you're hungry, I recommend hitting up Slice of Life diner. Try the apple-pie pancakes. I think you'll really like them.

I'm off to work. If you need something, give me a call.

Love you!

By the time I left, the sky was a brilliant blue. It went from a light, almost white color at the horizon to a deep navy overhead as the sun peeked out over the hilltop. I took the scenic route into town. Something about early-morning drives was peaceful, especially when I was driving through areas with no traffic. That was one of the many benefits of living on the outskirts of Point Pleasant.

I pulled up to a stop in front of Tina's home. The scent of burned wood hung heavy in the air around the house but had dissipated significantly in the surrounding blocks. Parked, blocking the driveway to the home, was a sheriff's patrol car.

I got out and walked toward the house. When I was about twenty feet away, a man in a deputy's uniform rounded the corner of the house. He gripped a roll of yellow caution tape, which trailed behind him. Chris had mentioned the department had hired a new deputy. We hadn't met yet. It made sense that they would assign him the grunt work, like putting up crime-scene caution tape. I forced a smile onto my face as I walked up the drive.

He straightened to his full height as I approached. I craned my head back as he went up and up and just kept going. He was at least 6'6" if not taller, and lanky. His limbs hung at his sides, gangly and somewhat awkward.

He waved at me, his hand the size of my face. "Good morning, ma'am."

I shielded my eyes as I peered up at him. He had blond hair clipped close to his head, with a matching goatee and hazel eyes. There was a youthfulness to his face. He was probably only a few years older than my daughter.

"Good morning. I'm here on behalf of the insurance company."

He shifted uncomfortably. "A Ms. Williams, right?"

"That's me. Has the scene been cleared yet? The fire investigator said it should be available today."

"I'm afraid not." He cleared his throat. "You'll need permission from Bob—I mean the sheriff—to get inside."

I peeked past him at the house. It was almost exactly the same. I squinted at the empty space where the tires had been. They must have been taken in for evidence. I nodded and retreated to my car, where I fidgeted with my phone. *Should I text Chris? He's much more likely to tell me what's going on than Bob is.* I gritted my teeth. This was for work. I need to go through the official channels first.

———

I pulled up outside the sheriff's office and stared out at the two faded double-wides propped on cinder blocks over a gravel parking lot. Over the fall, a storm had come through and ripped off the skirting around the main structure. It hadn't been replaced yet. That didn't surprise me much. Those manufactured structures were meant to be temporary locations while the main office downtown was being rebuilt after a major water loss. Four years later, they were still languishing on the outskirts of town. The gravel crunched under my feet as I strode toward the front door.

Inside, it wasn't much better. The whole building was dilapidated. The overhead lights flickered and hummed as I entered the room. Peggy looked up from behind her desk. She pushed her red cat-eye glasses up the bridge of her nose. Her hair had grown out some over the past few months, and she was wearing it in a graying shag that reminded me of Farrah Fawcett.

I smiled as I approached her desk. My resolve to go through proper channels melted under the power of her gaze. While she'd always been friendly toward me, she, like the sheriff, was displeased by my meddling in the last murder investigation.

I raised my hand in a weak wave. "Is Chris in?"

She pursed her lips. "He's out."

I fought the urge to fidget under her gaze. "Do you know—"

She held up a finger and picked up the phone on her desk. She jabbed in a number with her pen. "Ms. Williams is here to see you." She hung up. "Bob will be right out."

I backed away from the desk. While she did normally wear her disappointment on her sleeve, Peggy was terser than normal. I sat down on one of the plastic seats in the makeshift waiting room and stared at a corkboard filled with various community announcements. That fall was a quiet one. A poster for a missing dog took up most of the board. It was a cute Pomeranian with an impressive golden poof of fur for a chest. Written in large pink letters over her head were the words Princess Sparkle.

I studied every item on the board. Someone had painted the Miller farm's cow blue again. The reward for information on the culprit had been raised to one thousand dollars. I went from post to post and back again—not a single mention of trash fires. I shifted in my seat and reread the entire board again. By the time Bob made his appearance, I'd read the full life story of Princess Sparkle for the ninth time.

"Miss Williams." He didn't look at me as he spoke, instead staring at the newspaper in his hands.

"Good morning, Bob," I said. When he crooked an eyebrow, I cleared my throat. "Sheriff Wright. I was hired to inspect the property on Vanguard and wanted to know if I could get in there."

"No."

My eyes widened, and I suppressed an exacerbated gasp. I swallowed and put on my best professional smile. "Did the investigator find something? I have training on how not to disturb a scene."

"But apparently no training on how to keep things to yourself." He closed the paper and glared at me.

"What is that supposed to mean?"

"All this additional security wouldn't be necessary if you hadn't leaked it to the press." He thrust the paper toward me.

The fire was on the front page. A photo of the burned building took up half the page, and in big bold letters over the picture was the headline "Young Woman Murdered." Halfway down the page was an opinion piece titled "Has the Crime Wave Hit Our Community?" I blinked. *What does this have to do with me?*

He looked at me expectantly. I read through the article and paused at my name in the second paragraph. My eyes flicked between my name, the author, Isabelle Carter, and the photo. The quote wasn't incorrect. I'd directed her to the sheriff's office if she had questions. That was how things were done back in Spokane. *Is it not normal here? Will the entire town think I'm a gossip now?*

He jabbed his finger at the opinion piece. "This isn't Seattle. Or Spokane. This is a small town. Or have you forgotten? Whenever—and I mean whenever—there's any sort of crime here, people get overly excited. Which makes my job much more difficult. Do you have any idea how many calls we get asking for an update on the blue cow? Not tips but requests for updates."

"I'm sorry, I didn't realize it wasn't... public knowledge," I sputtered.

"Multiple times a day," he continued as if I hadn't spoken. "And that's just for the blue cow. This morning, we've had to field twenty-seven different calls on this case. That is precious time and resources we could spend doing something useful. In the future, *Ms. Williams*, if you hear about crime in the town, don't speak to the press."

"I didn't. I told her—"

"Told her that there was a homicide."

"I told her to speak to you. That's standard practice."

He glowered at me. "Not here."

I swallowed as he grabbed the newspaper out of my hand and turned to leave. "But…"

He craned his head toward me, scowling. "But?"

I dropped my hand. "Do you know when I'll be able to get in there?"

"Once we have made an arrest." He glanced behind me and glowered. "Luckily for you, we are bringing in the prime suspect right now."

Chris opened the front door with a scruffy man thrust in front of him. My eyes flicked between Chris and the suspect. While Chris was tall, dark, and handsome, the suspect was short, with a wild head of hair and a beard that stuck out in random directions. They shuffled past me. The suspect's clothes were dirty, and he picked at his grime-covered fingernails, his hands handcuffed in front of him. He wasn't much taller than me, maybe five feet seven at the most. I stared at their backs as they walked away.

I turned to stare at the sheriff, who had a triumphant gleam in his eyes.

"Are you sure you have the right guy?" I asked.

"He looks good for it." The sheriff rocked back on his heels and thrust his thumbs into his belt loops.

"I just… expected someone taller."

He squinted at me.

I coughed. "I took a statement from a neighbor. He said he saw someone leave the house earlier in the night, and… they were tall."

"By 'neighbor,' do you mean William Wallace?"

I nodded.

He snorted. "I wouldn't give much weight to what he has to say. Willy's a drunk. You can't rely on statements from people like him."

"He seemed—"

He raised a hand to cut me off. "This guy is a firebug, a homeless firebug who's banned from all but one shelter on the island, which we have confirmed he was not at. We've connected him to at least eight other fires in the area. See? Police work. You really should leave it to the professionals."

"The trash fires?"

"You could call them that."

I blinked at him, at a loss for words. He smirked and disappeared down the hallway after Chris. I stood there, frozen. Though some time had passed since my arson-investigation training, the section on disorganized fire starters always stuck out to me. People who started trash fires rarely graduated to house fires—at least, not on purpose. I doubted the findings had changed much over the years. *What am I missing here? Were they not just trash fires?*

After a minute, Chris came out of the room and walked toward me. He stopped a few feet away and gave me a stiff nod. "Ms. Williams."

I squinted at him and cocked my head to one side. *He's being oddly formal today.* "Can we talk for a second?"

He looked over at Peggy, nodded, and pulled me aside into the lobby, within view of her desk. "What can I help you with?"

"Are you okay?" I whispered.

He shifted uncomfortably and glanced back over at Peggy. He lowered his voice. "This is the first big case since Teresa passed away."

Teresa was the sheriff's wife. She'd lost her fight with cancer a few weeks earlier, and he hadn't taken it well.

"Oh, poor Bob." I glanced over at Peggy and inched closer. "I'm not sure if you have the right person."

He stiffened. "I can't discuss the case with you, Dani."

"Why not? You've told me about your work before."

"This is different." He glanced over at Peggy, who was staring straight at him. He inched away from me. "If there is nothing else, I should get back to work."

After the last case, Bob had punished him by putting him

on traffic duty despite him being a senior deputy. He was still stuck with that punishment, all these months later.

I clenched my teeth. "Are we on for coffee?"

His expression softened. "You bet. It's the highlight of my week."

I made a quick exit. If Bob was still on edge over Jessica and now Teresa, I didn't want to get Chris in worse trouble. This might be his first opportunity to get back into the sheriff's good graces. At least, I hoped that was the explanation for his cool behavior.

I climbed into my car and stared blankly out my windshield. *Now what?* I rechecked my email. No new claims had come in. I was fresh out of things to do. I smiled. *A silver lining, perhaps? At least I'll have time to spend with Grace today.*

CHAPTER 6

Charlie greeted me at the door and yowled until I picked him up. When he was a newborn kitten, he enjoyed nestling into my hair to sleep. He had grown, but he still wanted to be up. I grunted at the weight.

"Buddy, I'm not sure if we'll be able to do this for much longer."

He purred into my ear and kneaded at my shoulder, being careful not to scrape me with his claws.

"I missed you too." I scratched him behind his ears. "But I am super proud of you for taking care of my baby while she wasn't feeling well."

He meowed and rested his head on my shoulder. I carried him through the house, searching for Grace. I found her in her bedroom. She was sitting on the floor, sorting through a box of odds and ends that had been left in a corner. She'd changed out of her clothes from the previous night and was wearing flannel pajamas with her hair piled on top of her head in a loose, messy bun. She glanced up at me as she wiped sleep from the corner of her eye.

"I've got the rest of the day off." I leaned against the doorframe. "Why don't we do something together while you're in town? You up for a little adventure?"

Grace pulled an old cardigan out of the box. It was black, with red roses embroidered on the front. It was vintage, probably from the 1950s.

She turned it over in her hands and set it aside. "I'm moving in, remember? We have plenty of time to go do things."

"I know." I readjusted Charlie. "But why not take advantage of the time we've got today? It's nice out. What do you want to do?"

She shrugged.

"We could go to lunch... or a hike, maybe?"

"I'm tired." She pulled a cookbook out of the box next and flipped through it.

"Did you not get enough sleep last night?"

"I said I'm tired." She dropped the book in her lap and rubbed at the bridge of her nose. "I'm sorry. I haven't been sleeping well."

I opened my mouth, but no words came out. I closed it and chewed on my lip.

Grace looked up at me. Her brown eyes, so dark that her irises almost looked black, were red rimmed. "Can we stay in? Maybe... make this feel more like home? Everything still feels like Gran."

I crouched in front of her and picked up the book. It had the iconic white-and-red-checkered pattern of the Better Homes and Gardens cookbooks, although faded. As I touched it, a feeling of fatigue swept over me. I wobbled on my feet and tucked the book away. I forced a smile. "Then why don't we make it feel more like you?"

She sagged into the dresser behind her and let out a large breath. A slow smile spread across her lips, and she let out a shaky laugh. "That sounds wonderful, Mom."

"First things first. Let's get this box moved up to the attic. And then we can get you unpacked." I stood, lifting the box.

She scrambled up, grabbing the random assortment of items she'd taken out, and threw them inside the box. She followed me up the stairs, her head swiveling from doorway to doorway as we walked. "So why'd you pick the first-floor bedroom for me?"

I faltered as I took the next step. I hadn't given that much thought. In the back of my mind, I'd assumed it would be a temporary stay, and the first-floor bedroom had always been the guest room. *If she's really moving in, shouldn't she get to pick?* I stopped in the middle of the hallway, and Grace bumped into me.

"Why don't you pick?" I turned toward her.

Her smile widened. "Any of the rooms?"

I narrowed my eyes, giving her a mock suspicious look. "Any room except for mine."

She threw her head back and laughed. "The bedroom downstairs is right under yours, so I could hear you every time you got up in the middle of the night." She swiveled in place, studying the doorways. "How about this one?" She gestured toward the first door on the right.

Three bedrooms were on the top floor, the large master suite and two smaller rooms. Between the two on the left was a jack-and-jill bathroom connecting them. The bedroom she'd chosen had been mine every summer when I was growing up. After I went off to college, it had slowly filled with random odds and ends and was currently a storage room.

I poked my head into both bedrooms. My gran had become a pack rat over the past few years, and both had boxes stacked inside. But they were half empty, with plenty of room to move things around.

"Okay." I pursed my lips. "Let's clear it out."

Grace retrieved her laptop from downstairs and set up

streaming music to play while we worked. Charlie joined us and scampered about underfoot, batting a stuffed mouse around while we sorted through Gran's old things. At first, I took a quick peek in the boxes before we moved them, but that took too long. We carried a good fifty boxes of varying sizes from one bedroom to the other. When we ran out of space, we carted them up the attic steps. Each load reminded me of how much work the house still needed. The floorboards creaked. My foot more than once got caught on the edge of the frayed carpet before the attic stairs. I'd been so focused on finishing up my new office that I hadn't stopped to think about the house.

We were down to the last few boxes when Grace slowed and faltered. She sat down on the stairs, her head between her knees.

"You all right, sweetie?" I stopped and plopped down on the steps next to her on my way down.

"I'm getting tired."

I patted her on the shoulder. She stiffened under my hand then relaxed. "I can finish moving the boxes if you want to take a break."

She nodded but stayed slumped on the stairwell.

"We can always move your bed later. We should probably paint in there before we do anything else, anyway."

"And replace the carpet…"

I picked at the frayed carpet on the stairs. "Yeah. This whole house could use a facelift."

She rested her head against the wall. She smiled weakly. "I wasn't going to say anything, but yeah. It's…" She wrinkled her nose. "Dated."

I laughed.

She winced and rubbed her forehead. "I should probably go lie back down."

I studied her. "You've been sleeping a lot since you got here. Are you feeling okay?"

She rested her head on my shoulder. "I'll be okay."

"'Will be okay' and 'are okay' are two different things." I wrapped an arm around her.

She closed her eyes. "I'm just so worn out, you know? High school didn't prepare me for how hectic life on campus was going to be. I need time to recuperate. Get my reserves back up. I didn't expect everything to be so draining."

I squeezed her. "Are you sure you didn't catch something? Dorm life is like living in a petri dish. I can take you to a walk-in clinic if you want."

"No," she blurted and pulled away.

"Are you sure?" I reached for her, but she twisted away. My hand dropped to my lap.

She stood. "I'm tired. That's all."

"It's okay. Go rest. I'll finish up here. But promise me something?"

"What?" She peered at me over her shoulder.

"If there's something wrong, you'll tell me?"

She crossed her heart. "Good night, Mom. Love you."

Charlie looked between me and Grace as she walked away down the hall. He gave the stuffed mouse one last bat and followed Grace down the stairs. Things had been so much easier when she was small. *When did she stop telling me things?* I hung my head. *Probably around the time I stopped telling her things.* Trust was a two-way street, and I'd broken it with the divorce. *When I tell her about being a witch, will I ever be able to get that trust back?*

I sighed and pushed myself up. I marched up and down the hall, carrying the last few boxes up to the attic. After safely storing the last box, I switched off the lights and shuffled downstairs. Grace was passed out in her bed, softly snoring. Charlie lay curled up on her pillow, a single paw on Grace's shoulder. He stared at her sleeping face.

I tiptoed into the room and petted him. "You worried about her, bud?"

He slowly blinked at me and laid his head down next to her.

"Me too." I scratched him behind his ears.

I retreated to the living room and flopped down on the couch. My arms were sore from lifting all the boxes, but I was wide awake. I texted Heather.

> **DANI:**
> You still up for helping me bake cookies for the gift baskets?

> **HEATHER:**
> I've been brainstorming all day. Closing shop now. Come over so I can regale you with my cookie ideas.

I grinned. Heather loved baking almost as much as she loved cats and discovering new roasts.

> **DANI:**
> I'll be there in twenty.z

I groaned as I pushed myself off the couch, and my arms shook under my weight. I checked on Grace again, grabbed my purse, and shuffled out the door.

The windows of the Bizzy Bean were dark. I smiled at the Closed sign. Heather had changed it out too. It used to have a honeycomb pattern, but now it was an illustration of a sleeping cat with a bee flying overhead and spelling "Closed" with its flight path. It was adorable. She really was leaning into merging the two themes.

I peered inside. Heather was wiping down the last table. I rapped my knuckles on the glass, and she let me in.

As the door opened, she glanced down at my feet, and her face fell. "No Charlie?"

I shook my head. "He's acting as a nurse for Grace."

"When did she get in? I thought she wasn't arriving until next week."

"She arrived early. She appeared on my doorstep last night, bag in hand, and announced she was moving in."

"Oh gosh. Is she doing okay?"

"I don't know." I followed Heather through the cafe to the hidden stairwell at the back. "She said school really exhausted her. She's been sleeping a lot. I'm worried about her."

Star greeted us at the top of the stairs and pranced around our feet. After she went around me once, she stopped. Her head swiveled around, searching for Charlie. She looked straight up at me and let out a low grumble. She backed away, lifted her tail straight up, and walked away with her head held high.

We followed Star into the apartment. Over the years, Heather had renovated it. She'd knocked down several walls to make room for a much larger kitchen than the townhome had originally allowed. Half of the great room was dedicated to cooking. Floor-to-ceiling cabinets covered one wall. A long L-shaped quartz counter swept along the back and side wall, and in the center was an island so large you could serve Thanksgiving dinner on it. The living room, in comparison, barely had enough space for her couch and TV. Overhead was her bedroom loft.

Star sauntered over to a playpen in the corner. She gave me one last indignant look and jumped inside. I peered over the edge. Inside were eleven kittens, all between eight and fourteen weeks old. Heather must have been given a second litter.

I raised an eyebrow at Heather.

"They're only going to be here a few days. I swear!"

"A few days, huh?" I put my hands on my hips.

"The shelter called and didn't have room for them. But

they're lining up another foster while we speak. I'm only going to have the first set for adoption downstairs."

As Star moved from kitten to kitten, grooming them, I smiled. "If it takes more than a few days, it won't be so bad."

Heather playfully swatted at me. She walked into the kitchen, pulling out a wooden cardholder labeled Cookies. She flipped through the cards, pausing in a few different places to pull out cards. "I had four in mind that are perfect for this time of year." She slid the cards across the counter toward me.

I read the names. "Peppermint spritz, peanut butter blossoms, frosted pumpkin, and Italian wedding." My mouth watered.

"They sound amazing." I slid the cards back across the counter. "Where do we start?"

She grabbed totes from under the counter. "I may have measured out ingredients while I was on my lunch break."

When the first batch came out of the oven, I leaned over the counter and inhaled deeply. The cookies had a subtle peppermint scent, mixed with the classic sweetness of a sugar cookie. "They smell amazing." I straightened, admiring our work. "Oh. How did the health inspection go?"

"I haven't heard yet." She put the next batch of cookies into the oven. "I'm not too worried about it, though. I keep a clean kitchen and have maintained an A-plus rating for years. How about you? How did your home inspection go this morning?"

I slumped. "It didn't."

"What happened?"

"The tenant was murdered, and now I'm barred from the scene by the sheriff."

She gasped. "For how long?"

I stared down at the floor and fidgeted with my foot. "Until they make an arrest."

"That's... Oooh. Sheriff Wright can be so frustrating sometimes. Do they at least have a suspect?"

"Yeah. One." I bit my lip.

"Why do I feel like there's a *but* coming?"

I shrugged.

She stepped in front of me to catch my gaze. "Dani?"

I exhaled and looked up as her eyes burrowed into me. I never could hide things from her for long. "I think they have the wrong person."

She nodded and took a step back. She leaned against the counter, crossing her arms across her stomach, waiting for me to continue.

I paced as I told her about my conversation with the neighbor and the sheriff. I couldn't tell her about the impression I'd gotten from the tree. She wouldn't understand. I held my arms out at my sides. "It could mean nothing, right? He's an unreliable witness."

"Do you think he's an unreliable witness?"

"The sheriff—"

"I didn't ask what Bob thinks. I asked what you think."

I lowered my arms. "I don't know."

"Why don't you interview him again and decide for yourself?"

"I'm not supposed to—"

"Inspect the property. He didn't say anything about talking to people."

I grinned. "I suppose if I can't get into the house until they make an arrest, I might as well try to help nudge their investigation along."

She met my grin with one of her own. "Exactly."

I laughed. "Why, Ms. Bellerose, are you being a bad influence on me?"

She opened her mouth in a mock offended expression. "I would never."

My body vibrated in anticipation. All day, I'd felt directionless with the claim, but now, I had something to do, someplace to go.

"I can handle baking the rest of the cookies if you want to see if you can catch the neighbor before he goes to work."

I eyed the cookies on the counter behind her.

"Yes, you can take some with you to warm him up."

"Thank you." I grabbed the plate.

"Just update me!" She yelled as I dashed down the stairs. "And don't do anything dangerous!"

CHAPTER 7

On the darkened street, the burned wreckage blended in with the night. Only the corner of the house was visible from a streetlight down the block. It stood out more because of the sudden darkness. All the other homes had porch lights or a lingering warmth from lights peeking out the edges of curtained windows. The scent hung heavy in the air, burning the nose.

I paused on the sidewalk outside the house, squinting up at it. A car passed, its headlights catching on the yellow caution tape. I walked across the street to the neighbor's house. His car was parked in the driveway. I readjusted the plate of cookies and knocked on the front door.

Inside, feet fell against the wooden floors. As I stood shivering in the dark, I whispered the words to a spell that transformed the cookies into an edible relaxation potion. It would make whoever ate them feel comfortable. The warm light of the spell floated down onto them and settled in, and the cookies glowed on the plate. Fortunately, I was the only one who could see the magic.

Willy cracked the door open. He peeked out at me from

behind the chain. "You're the adjuster from earlier, aren't you? What do you want?"

"I have a few more questions, if you have a minute."

He shook his head and started closing the door. "I'm getting ready for work."

I leaped forward and lifted the plate of cookies so that he could see them before the door shut all the way. "I brought cookies for your time. It'll only take a minute."

His eyes flicked between my face and the plate. "What type?"

"Peppermint spritz. Fresh from the oven."

"I haven't had those cookies in ages. I used to love them, growing up." He closed the door, the chain rattled, and it reopened. "I've got to get ready, but we can chat while I pack up my dinner."

I followed him into the kitchen. The house was a little worn around the edges but clean. The furniture was dated. He probably hadn't bought any new pieces since the nineties. He bustled around the kitchen, making coffee and packing up a sandwich for the evening. Except for the coffee, everything about the lunch box seemed like something I would've packed for my daughter in grade school. His meal comprised a peanut-butter-and-jelly sandwich, apple slices, a bag of Goldfish crackers, and a fun-sized Snickers. The counters were mostly bare. As he worked, he seemed to have only one cutting board, knife, and plate—a true bachelor. The only thing out of place was a bag of kids' toys, still in their packaging, next to the fridge.

"I know we went over this already, but I hoped you could tell me about what you saw again."

He cut his sandwich into quarters and slid it into Tupperware. He didn't look at me while he spoke. "Why are you asking?"

"When we spoke yesterday morning, you seemed a little... upset. Did you know Tina well?"

51

He shook his head and continued working. He sprinkled lemon juice on the apple slices. I studied him as he worked. His shoulders were rolled forward, and his eyes darted around the room at everything but me. I pursed my lips. *I need you to talk to me.*

"You should try the cookies while they're still warm." I set the plate down next to him and pulled back the cling film.

He grabbed one off the plate and nibbled at the corner. He made an appreciative sound and grabbed a second. I waited for him to finish eating. The light from the spell seeped into his skin, and he glowed softly. The first time I saw the spell take hold, it had startled me, but I'd grown accustomed to it.

"We only started talking over the past month. I started doing yard work. I know. It's late in the year. But it had gotten pretty overgrown. I was pulling the weeds out of the flower bed when she came out. She was... sweet. She reminded me of my daughter when she was that age."

"She's around my daughter's age. As a mother, it hits too close to home. I just want to know what happened." I placed my hand over his. When he looked at me, I held his gaze. "Don't you?"

"I do."

"Then tell me. What did you see the night of the fire?"

He went over everything he'd seen that night, not leaving any details out. It was basically the same statement he'd told me that morning but in a lot more detail.

"Did you tell the sheriff about this?"

"Yes." His face reddened, and he lowered his gaze. "He isn't willing to give me a shot."

"Why's that?"

"I haven't always been reliable. But I'm working on it." Willy pulled his hand back and fished around in his pocket. He pulled out a chip and set it on the counter. "Three months and nine days sober. I know what I saw last night."

I picked up the chip and stared at it. As I touched it, pride mixed with shame washed over me—pride over making it so far and shame for having the problem to begin with.

"That's great, Willy."

He puffed out his chest and picked up one of the toys from the counter. He turned it over in his hands, his eyes becoming misty. "I have a grandson. He's almost four. I haven't been able to see him yet. But my daughter promised me a supervised visit at Christmas if I can stay sober. I won't jeopardize that for nothing."

I slid the AA chip toward him over the counter and thanked him for his time.

After I left, I sat in my car, staring at the dark space on the street where the burned-out house stood. I bit my lip. The sheriff was wrong. Someone left her house the night of the fire, someone tall. And that someone was definitely not the man the sheriff had in custody.

Who is the man they have in custody? I pulled out my phone and searched through the few articles I could find online. His name wasn't mentioned anywhere, and I found only one brief mention of a person of interest. I punched in Chris's number but hit Cancel before dialing. He might not tell me anything, not after the fiasco with the reporter. *The reporter?*

I grinned and scrolled through my call history until I found her number. I gripped the phone, my knuckles turning white. With each ring, I whispered "pick up" under my breath.

She picked up on the seventh ring. Her voice was wary.

"Do you know who the suspect is?" I asked.

"Umm, I... Who is this?" she stuttered.

"Danielle Williams. You quoted me in your article this morning."

She was silent for a few seconds. I held my breath, waiting for her to continue.

"Your article got me banned from the scene. I can't get in there to do my job. I want to know the case is on track so I can keep my client happy."

"I don't know if—"

"Please. You owe me for getting me kicked out."

She sighed. Papers rustled in the background as she spoke. "His name is Clint Hastings. They have connected him to a few nuisance fires over the past few months—trash burning, that sort of thing."

"Do you know where he's currently staying?"

"It's not confirmed."

"But…?"

"I heard he has been staying at the Haven of Hope shelter in Oak Harbor."

I thanked her profusely and hung up. The possibilities rolled around in my head. People were more likely to answer questions in person, so calling them was out. I googled their hours. They were open until eleven, and it was two minutes after ten. Oak Harbor was on the northern half of the island, an almost fifty-minute drive one way. If I left right then, I would get there just before they closed.

I threw my phone onto the passenger seat and drove.

Haven of Hope was on Pioneer Way. It reminded me of the Marine View Drive from Point Pleasant. It wound its way along Skagit Bay. The roadway was lined with two-story painted brick buildings. Haven of Hope was in a corner lot with a mural of helping hands painted on one side.

I ducked through the door with only a few minutes left to spare. The room was mostly empty. The only person inside was a pink-haired receptionist who sat behind glass, drinking from a large steaming thermos. Muffled voices echoed to me from down a hall—a woman was trying to hold back a laugh as she chastised children squealing that they didn't want to go to bed yet.

I rubbed my hands against my pant leg and inched toward the desk. *Would she tell me anything?* My eyes flicked between her and her thermos. I whispered the words to the spell that would change her drink into a relaxation potion. *I really need to expand my repertoire. When Grace is out of the house, I should try to find the next journal again.*

The motes of light from the spell settled into her beverage. As she sipped it, the light seeped into her skin until she softly glowed under the fluorescent lights. I came to a stop in front of her.

She looked up, smiling. "Welcome to the Haven of Hope. What can I help you with today?"

I put my hands on the counter. "Is this where Clint Hastings normally stays?"

"Yes. Almost every night. I haven't seen him today, though. Is he okay?"

"He's being held on suspicion of arson."

She blinked and leaned back. "Arson? Are you sure? He's always been such a nice, quiet guy."

"He is. I was wondering—you said almost every night. Would you be able to check to see if he was here the night of the fire?"

She sat up straight and pulled her keyboard toward herself. "What date?"

I told her the date and held my breath as she typed it into her system. She frowned at the screen, her eyes darting between me and it.

"What's your involvement in this? Are you a cop?"

"No." I fished a business card out of my bag and slid it under the glass. "I'm a claims adjuster, investigating the fire on behalf of the insurance company. I'm just trying to figure things out, you know?"

She still had the subtle glow. It swirled under the skin, fighting against her suspicious nature. "Okay. That makes sense," she said after a few seconds. "He didn't sleep here that night."

I slumped against the counter. I didn't know what I'd been expecting, but I'd hoped to find something, anything that would clear his name. I was naïve to think I could find something so easily.

"We couldn't let him in," she continued. "He missed curfew."

My head jerked up. *Missed curfew?*

"He arrived twenty minutes too late. I had to turn him away. I felt so awful about it. All the buses were running late that day. I had to say no to at least eight of our usual residents. But the rules are the rules. I couldn't... I wanted to, but I couldn't break them."

"What time is curfew?"

"Ten thirty."

"So he was here at ten fifty?" I held my breath.

She nodded.

A grin spread across my face. The fire started at about eleven. Clint could never have made it back in time to start the fire. And he couldn't have been the guy under the tree, either. The timeline didn't add up. Clint was innocent.

I was too excited to notice the cold when I stepped back outside. I half walked, half jogged to my car to get someplace private and make a call. I dialed the sheriff's tip line and left a message. Clint had an alibi. And now the sheriff's office knew, it was only a matter of time before he was released.

CHAPTER 8

The next morning, I was still buzzing with energy. I forced my hands to remain steady as I poured my coffee. Clint was innocent. I'd given the sheriff the information they needed to clear his name. *Now what?*

I shuffled to my home office and logged into my system. I held my breath as my email loaded, half hoping a new claim would be in my inbox to distract me and half hoping nothing would be there.

The one and only new message was from the property manager. My heart raced as I opened it: "Received. Do you need anything from us in the meantime?"

I sighed and set my cup down. Chuckling, I shook my head. I typed a quick response, asking for pre-loss photos and a copy of the rental agreement, and I slumped into my chair.

I sipped my coffee, staring at the blank screen over the rim of my mug. I didn't know anything about Tina. With Jessica, a friend whose murderer I'd helped capture, I'd had some place to start. I knew her. I knew who her friends were and what big events she had going on in her life. Tina was a blank page.

I went through the things I knew about her. She was young, only a few years older than my daughter. And... that was it. I pulled up the news articles on the fire and scanned them for additional details. She was a student at a local community college. She was an only child. Her parents wanted people to donate to a children's hospital in lieu of buying flowers. *Why that hospital? Did she stay there?*

A door slammed shut. My head jerked toward the sound. The floorboard creaked in the hallway. I gripped the edge of my chair, staring at the door. Grace poked her head around the corner, her dark-brown hair disheveled.

I chuckled, releasing my hold on my armrest. "You startled me."

She rubbed her eyes. "What time is it?"

"Almost ten. You just now getting up?"

She stretched. Yawning, she nodded and flopped into a chair across from me.

I studied her. She'd slept for almost sixteen hours straight, but that had done nothing to combat the dark circles under her eyes.

"Are you feeling okay?"

She rolled her eyes.

I held up my hands. "A mother's allowed to be worried. It feels like you've been sleeping more than you're awake."

She focused on her hands as she picked at her nails. "I'm exhausted from school. I'm sure I'll be fine in a few more days."

The hairs on my arms stood up as a tingling sensation I associated with the Sight washed over me. I chewed on my lip. "Is... is that why you dropped out? Was school making you tired?"

She glowered at me and stood up. "I need to take a shower."

"Did I tell you about my first claim?"

58

"You can tell me about it later." She strode toward the door.

She was almost out of the room. The tingling sensation hadn't gone away.

"It involves a murder," I blurted.

She paused in the doorway. "A murder?"

"Yeah. It's early days, but it looks like someone might have burned the house down to hide it."

She glanced at me over her shoulder.

I shifted in my chair. "The sheriff is bungling the investigation too."

She chuckled, a wry smile on her lips. "Let me guess—you think you could do better?"

I pursed my lips. "I don't know. Maybe? I know nothing about her."

"Have you talked to her friends?"

"No—"

She leaned against the doorjamb, her arms crossed. "Why not? Friends almost always know what's going on in someone's life."

"You're right."

I pulled my laptop closer and searched for Tina on social media. Finding her profile didn't take long. Charlie jumped up onto my desk and flopped onto his side. I scratched his chin as I scrolled through her profile. Her friends list was over four hundred people long.

"She has a lot of friends."

Grace moved behind me, hovering over my shoulder. "Look at her check-ins."

When I moved my hand to type, Charlie latched onto my wrist and pulled my hand back.

"Easy, buddy." I winced as his claws scraped my skin. I extricated my hand and tried to type again. In response, Charlie flopped across my keyboard.

Grace laughed and plucked him from the desk. She

cradled him against her chest and played with him while I worked.

I scrolled through Tina's check-ins. Post after post had the same two names, Tina Monroe and Katie Cole. I stopped at a post from three months prior. The two girls sat outside a brick building, their heads tilted toward each other. Their smiles were wide but tired. While Katie was pretty, Tina was stunning. Her light-brown hair hung in waves around her shoulders. Her green eyes were bright and shone like she had been caught midlaugh.

I clicked on Katie's profile. Most of her posts were private, but a few pieces of information were public. Katie and Tina both worked for the Pacific Northwest Community College, in the financial aid office.

Grace peered over my shoulder. "You should talk to her."

"You think so?" I hid my smile.

She seemed to have the curiosity gene too. "Best friends and coworkers? There's no way she doesn't know something useful."

I looked up the phone number for their office.

"You want some tea?" Grace asked.

"Yes, please!"

Grace disappeared into the kitchen. I dialed the office and set up an appointment for later in the day. Satisfied, I reclined in my chair and stared at the screen.

Grace's words came back to me. Friends almost always know what's going on in someone's life. I glanced at the open doorway. In the kitchen, cups clinked against the counter. The kettle was heating but hadn't boiled yet. She would be out of the room for a few more minutes.

I pulled up Grace's profile and scrolled. Since the start of the semester, her posts had become more and more sporadic. Her twice-a-day habit had gone down to one, then every other day to maybe once a week. The kettle whistled in the kitchen. I glanced toward the door and continued scrolling.

The last time Grace had checked in was over a month before. That was with one of her high school friends, Madison. She was a good kid. They were in track and field together, and she'd crashed at our house more than once after an all-night study session over the years. I clicked on Madison's profile. She also went to Gonzaga.

The floorboard creaked in the hall. I closed the search window and turned, smiling, as Grace came in. My palms were sweaty as I accepted my drink.

CHAPTER 9

Pacific Northwest Community College was a short ferry ride across the bay in Mukilteo. I spent the ride over studying Tina's social media for clues. In her posts, she seemed happy and hopeful about the future. There were lots of cute videos of her singing along to popular music, along with food photos and with the occasional meme thrown into the mix. She liked puns and grumpy cats. It was all impersonal, at least publicly.

The community college was tucked away in a quiet corner of the city. At first glance, it barely looked like a college. Half the buildings seemed almost residential from the outside. The school's website said someone had donated them to the college in the 1950s. The other half were a hodgepodge of new architecture and brick structures almost like storefronts. I pulled into one of the campus's newest structures, the parking garage, and made my way over to the quad.

All the administrative offices were in the main house. My breath caught as I entered the building. It was a gorgeous plantation-style house with marble floors and intricate wood detailing.

I glanced at my watch. My meeting with Katie was in less than a minute. I strode up the stairs two at a time and marched down the hall, passing small clusters of students huddled outside various offices, waiting to be seen. I came to a stop outside the financial aid office and ran my fingers through my hair to smooth down any flyaways.

Straightening, I pushed the door open and peered inside. The office was quiet inside, and the only sound was the clicking of a keyboard. I stepped into the office, which was smaller than I'd expected. Only two workstations sat behind a long, thin counter with two doors behind, one leading to a meeting room and the other to a darkened office. Katie was the only one in the room.

She glanced up at me as I approached the desk. "You must be my two o'clock. Dani, right?"

I nodded.

She smiled, but it didn't fully reach her eyes. Sadness was there instead. "It's too late in the semester to get started for the next term. When were you or your child looking to enroll?" The word *child* rose like a question.

"I'm actually here about another matter."

"Oh?"

I pressed my hands against the counter to stop them from shaking. She didn't have to talk to me. I didn't have a good reason to be here in any official capacity. "I'm an insurance adjuster, working on a claim for a property management company. They own the house Tina lived in."

Her face fell. "Oh."

"I am so sorry for your loss. I understand you two were close, and I was hoping you might help me."

She swallowed and stood. "It was about time for my break, anyway. Mind if we grab a cup of coffee while we talk?"

"Not at all."

She grabbed her purse, and I followed her out. She

flipped a sign on the door saying Be Back in 15 Minutes and locked the door behind us.

I kept pace with her as she strode down the stairs and made her way over to the campus coffee stand. It was built out of a single piece of curved granite that took up the entire back wall of the student lounge. Once upon a time, it had been a sitting room. The only things that remained to reveal its past identity were the big bay windows and bricked-over fireplace. Scattered through the room were small tables and cushioned chairs, with over half the tables taken by students studying for their midterm exams. We got our drinks and settled at an open table in the corner.

"How are you holding up?" I asked.

"I don't know, to be honest. Devastated. Shocked. Is it true someone murdered her?"

"It's early in the investigation." I studied her face while I spoke, seeing a hopelessness in her eyes, which was replaced with determination as I continued. "But I want to find out. And I need your help to do so."

Katie inched forward in her seat, her coffee forgotten on the table. "What do you need to know?"

"Do you know if there were any recent changes in her life?"

"She... she broke up with her boyfriend recently. Do you think he might have had something to do with it?"

"Maybe. How did he take it?"

She gripped the edge of the table, her face pinched. "Tina was always a little secretive about her love life. She never said anything, but she stopped taking his calls, and last week, I noticed she was having campus security walk her to her vehicle. When I asked her about it, she laughed it off and told me—" Her voice cracked. "She told me I worry too much."

I grabbed a packet of tissues from my bag and held it out to her. She thanked me as she took one and dabbed at the corner of one eye.

"You were a good friend."

"I should have done more." She sobbed.

"There was no way for you to know something like this would happen. And we don't know if it was him." My words sounded hollow even to me.

It was sad, but it was far too common for the significant other to be the murderer in situations like this. Despite that, my words had an impact. Her sobbing stopped.

"But I should probably still talk to him. Do you know how I might be able to find him?"

"He's probably on campus. His name is Samuel Koenig. He used to call so frequently I have his phone number memorized." She wrote it down for me. "I've got to get back to work. Did you have any other questions before I go?"

"Was she close to anyone else? Is there someone else you think I should talk to?"

"Our boss. But he left early for the day. If you find something, you'll tell me, right?"

"Of course."

She jotted down her number then made her way across the room and disappeared back up the stairs, her shoulders slumped. I sipped at my coffee. If the breakup had been a nasty one, then the boyfriend was a good lead. I chewed my lip. *But wouldn't the sheriff have looked into him first? Maybe they didn't know. Or didn't find anything...*

I checked social media to see if I could track him down, but he wasn't on her friends list. Three viable matches had some variation of Samuel and Koenig as a last name in the area. Without knowing what he looked like, I couldn't tell which one was him.

I replayed the conversation in my head again.

Campus security had walked her to her car. Maybe they would know something. Smiling, I stood and made my way over to the coffee stand. With the steady drizzle outside, he would be cold. A nice warm drink would probably get him talking.

On such a small campus, tracking down security wasn't hard. The guard huddled under the parking garage overhang. I pulled my coat tight around myself and trudged toward him, my head bent into the wind. When I was twenty paces away, I muttered the words to the spell that would change the coffee into a relaxation potion. Nothing happened. I faltered and repeated the words, forcing meaning into them. Shimmering lights floated from my mouth and into the cup. A wave of exhaustion hit me. I hadn't cast so many spells that close together before, and the effort was taking its toll. I pushed my shoulders back, and I ducked under the overhang with a smile.

The guard slapped his hands together and stomped his feet. "Good afternoon, ma'am."

I peered at his name tag. "Hi, Brian."

He gave me a puzzled look, glanced at his name tag, and chuckled. "Is there something I can help you with?"

"No… actually, this is probably silly. I was meeting with Katie, in the financial aid office, over coffee and, well, the barista accidentally made one too many drinks. She mentioned how cold it gets out here and how much she appreciates all you do… and, well, suggested I bring the extra out to you." I smiled awkwardly and held the coffee cup toward him. "She thought you might appreciate something warm."

A grin spread across his face as he took the coffee. "That's sweet of her. She's a great kid."

I sipped at my drink and watched him as the spell settled in. That gentle glow seeped into his skin as he drank the coffee.

"She really is. It honestly surprised me to see her at work. I was almost certain she would cancel our appointment after losing a friend so suddenly like that."

"It was heartbreaking hearing about Tina. She reminded me of my daughter at that age."

"Mine's only a few years behind. It's so scary. I hope they find her killer soon. From what I've heard, the only problem she had with anyone was her ex-boyfriend, so hopefully, it will be an open-and-shut case."

His gaze flicked away from me, and he hunched his shoulders.

"Did she have issues with someone else?" I asked.

"It wasn't her ex she was worried about." He looked around again and stepped in close to whisper. "For the last few weeks, some guy had been following her. She didn't know who he was, but he gave her the creeps."

I couldn't help thinking of Grace while I was digging into Tina's murder. Heat rose up the sides of my face as I imagined someone following my daughter. "Did you ever see him?"

"Only once."

"Do you remember what he looked like?" I clenched my jaw.

"I'll do you one better." He fished in his pocket and pulled out his cell phone. "I got a picture of him. It's a little blurry, but you can see him well enough."

I peered over his shoulder at the photo. The man was soft in the middle, with a rumpled button-up shirt. He had a goatee and a balding head. He was thoroughly average, almost too average. He could've been anyone, an absent-minded professor or a new father.

"Can you send that to me?"

"Yeah."

I gave him my email address. As I wandered back toward the student union building, questions swirled through my mind. *Who was the mystery man? What did he want with Tina? Is he connected to the ex somehow?* If not, this threw some serious doubt on the "it was the ex" theory I'd been operating on. I chewed on my lip as I walked. Only one way to find out—time to call Samuel Koenig.

CHAPTER 10

I counted the rings. After the fourth, I expected his voicemail to pick up any second. With all the robocalls these days, few people checked their voicemail. *Is it worth leaving a message?* I ran through what I was going to say.

He picked up on the eleventh ring. "Hello?"

I blinked. Everything I'd planned on saying vanished from my head.

"Hello?" Annoyance crept into his voice.

"Hi. My name is Dani Williams, with Williams Insurance Adjusting. I'm working on a claim for a recent fire loss. I was hoping I could ask you a few questions about Tina."

Silence greeted me. For a second, I thought he'd hung up. I held my breath, waiting for him to respond.

"I'm at the library," he said finally.

"On campus? I'm outside the student union building right now."

"Oh. Well, I'm going to be here for a few more minutes if you want to talk in person." He told me which room he was in and hung up.

I spun in place and pictured the campus map I'd found online. A good sense of direction was an important skill for claims adjusters to develop. Over the years, I'd had many claims in remote locations where my GPS didn't work. I overlaid the map in my mind and dashed toward the library.

It was housed in one of the buildings that had been added to the campus in the seventies. It was all hard angles and glass, with blocky rooms overhanging a small stylized garden. I half walked, half jogged to the building, only slowing as I approached the doors. I smoothed my hair before entering.

I followed the signs to the study rooms. I recognized him from one of the three profiles I'd found online. He was standing at the table, packing his laptop into his backpack.

I sighed and stepped into the room empty-handed. I was all out of coffee or cookies to help put him at ease. Plus, after how exhausted I felt after the last spell, I wasn't sure if I had another one in me. Cursing under my breath, I forced a sad smile onto my face. "Samuel Koenig?"

He froze in place and peered up at me.

"I'm Dani. We spoke on the phone."

"Right." He continued to pack up his belongings. The books in his bag weren't organized at all, and he struggled to stuff the last of his belongings into it.

"You have my condolences for your loss. If you wouldn't mind, I just had a few questions for you about her home."

He slumped and sank into his chair. "It's hard to believe she's really gone."

I slipped into the seat across from him and studied his down-turned face. "I understand you were pretty close."

"*Were* is an accurate descriptor." He snorted, shaking his head. He peered up at me and held my gaze. "We weren't together long, but it stung when she broke it off. I have to admit I half expected us to get back together someday."

"It must have been a shock when you found out."

"I was probably the last to know. Bartending leads to odd work hours. I had to find out at work when someone flipped past the evening news." He blinked back tears and stared up at the ceiling. "I'm not surprised, though. Being the last to know, I mean. It isn't exactly new with Tina."

"Was she a private person, then?"

He reached for his last book and fiddled with the other books in his bag, trying to find a good place for it. "What can I help you with?"

"Well, like I said, I'm working on the fire claim. I'm trying to put together an estimate for the repairs and wanted to know if she had made any recent changes to the home." I pulled out a rough diagram I'd put together based on photos from Zillow.

He pursed his lips as he studied the diagram. He pointed at the bedroom walls on the second floor. "She repainted a few months ago."

"Thanks. So, no structural changes?"

He shook his head.

"Thank you." I folded the diagram and slipped it back into my bag. "Do you know if she was having problems with anyone? Can you think of someone who might have wanted to hurt her?"

His whole body became rigid. He clenched his jaw and stared straight ahead. "Everyone liked Tina. I can't think of anyone who would want to hurt her."

I didn't need the tickle at the back of my mind to tell me he was lying. I studied him as I debated pushing the question.

"I've got to go." He surged to his feet and grabbed his backpack. He glanced down at the stray book in his hand and tucked it under his arm.

My next words died in my throat as he strode out of the room. I stared after him as he disappeared down the hall. I sank into my chair. While not foolproof, I had a good sense of when people were lying to me. When he said he was the last to know, that didn't feel like he was lying. But he clearly knew something about someone wanting to hurt her. *Did he know who the stalker was?*

My trip across the bay had left me with more questions than answers. I rested my hip against the ferry railing and stared out at the water. An unknown man had left Tina's house the night of her murder. *Who was it? Sam? The mysterious stalker?* I chewed my lip. *Who else might know something?*

I inhaled sharply as an idea formed. *The ferry.* Tina would've taken it every day to get to the school. Maybe the crew knew their regulars. I headed into the cafeteria and scanned the faces of the workers. The cafeteria was bustling with activity this time of day. I stopped when I saw one I'd spoken to before.

I made my way toward her. I kept my eyes locked on her dark-brown hair, cropped short into an asymmetric bob with the long sections tucked behind her ears, so that I wouldn't lose her in the crowded room. She was wiping down a table in the back.

I cleared my throat as I stepped up to the table. She looked up and smiled. "Dani!"

"Gwen! It's good to see you again. You got a quick second?"

She nodded as she moved over to the next table to wipe it down. She worked slowly, wiping the same section a few times before moving on. "I don't have long. What do you need?"

I pulled out my phone and showed her a picture of Tina. "Do you recognize her?"

"Grande, quad, nonfat, one-pump, no-whip mocha. I haven't seen her in a few days, though."

"She… She's dead."

Gwen gasped and covered her mouth. "How? When? What happened?"

"Her home burned to the ground. It looks like she might have been dead before the fire, though." I lowered my voice and stepped in closer. "Someone murdered her."

She sat down and blinked back a tear. "She was a bit of a diva, but she was always nice. Always left a good tip."

I sat down across from her and put a hand over hers, giving it a quick squeeze. "I'm working on the house fire claim. It's surreal. I'm trying to get the claim wrapped up, but it's needling at me, not knowing who did it."

"What can I do to help?"

"Do you know if she had problems with anyone while on board?"

She leaned toward me over the table, and her words came out almost like a stage whisper. "The opposite, in fact. At least once a week, she met with this guy. He looked too old for her, but it was clear they were involved. The way she looked at him… It was love."

I opened the picture of the mysterious man the security guard had sent me and showed it to her. "Was it this guy?"

She shook her head.

I quickly opened Samuel Koenig's profile and showed her his photo. She shook her head again.

"What did he look like?" I asked.

"Tall. Handsome. Brown hair. They would meet out on the balcony, so I never saw him up close."

"When's the last time you saw them together?"

"Probably about a week and a half ago. It was the last time I saw her. She looked happy. Very happy." She glanced up at a woman with beach-blond hair hovering a few feet away, waiting for the table, and stood up. "I've got to get back to work. Is there anything else I can do to help?"

"Have you seen him since?"

She shook her head and retreated from the table.

The ferry slowed as it approached the dock. Katie had said Tina didn't talk much about her love life. *Was she secretive because it was complicated or because it was prolific?* I gritted my teeth and stood. Tall with brown hair—definitely not Clint. No one would describe him as good-looking or tall. It wasn't Sam or the stalker. It was another one. The number of mysterious men was multiplying quickly.

CHAPTER 11

I spent the entire drive home pondering the case. My thoughts went in the same loop until I had to shake myself and force my mind to think about something else. I didn't have enough information, and worrying away at it wasn't doing anyone any good. I switched gears and instead thought about my daughter.

University had exhausted me, but it had also been thrilling. The adrenaline, the pressure, mixed with the excitement over a new chapter of my life, carried me through each semester until graduation. Standing on that stage, with my bachelor's of political science in hand, was one of my happiest moments. Grace hadn't made it through one semester without crumbling. Maybe sending her to a school so close to home had been a mistake. Maybe she was missing the excitement part. I chewed on my lip as I pulled into the driveway.

I paused and blinked at the empty space. Grace's car was gone.

I ambled into the house and peeked into her room. Her bags were piled in a corner. One of the dresser drawers was half closed. It couldn't shut all the way around the pile of T-shirts that had been shoved inside.

She was out of the house. I smiled. With how much she'd been sleeping lately, it was good that she was out exploring.

I have the house to myself.

I froze in the doorway as the realization sank in. Finally, I had time to practice my magic. Maybe the journal contained a spell that would be useful for the investigation. While I'd read the whole thing, keeping all the options straight in my head was hard. I fetched the journal from my bag and flipped through the pages, reading the various options.

Almost everything required access to a physical object. I couldn't get into the scene of the fire, and all the useful items would be locked up in the evidence room by then. I paused over one of the more complicated variants of experiencing an object's past. It didn't require the object itself, but it required access to the space where something had happened.

It was a purposeful activation of the Sight, which was my family's ability to see things that had happened or could happen in the future. It was unreliable and fragmented but had the potential to show something useful. *Would sitting across the street be close enough? If I have a clear line of sight into the backyard, would I be able to see who left that night?* It was a crapshoot. I didn't understand the Sight well enough, and Gran's written description of it almost made it sound like it had a will of its own: "The Sight will show you what you need to know." *Who decided what I need to know?* "This ritual works best with a polished obsidian mirror." I sighed and dropped the journal into my lap.

"Great, Gran. Where am I supposed to get that?" I muttered.

I shook my head, sat up, and continued reading. A bowl of water also worked as a focus. That I could do.

My palms became clammy, and my heartbeat quickened. I swallowed, trying to push down a lump in my throat. *Am I really going to do this? Activate my Sight?* The first time it had fully activated, I saw my friend Jessica dead. It was always on, in a way, in my subconscious. The tingles and emotions I picked up when I touched objects was the Sight, but it wasn't fully activated. When it was, it was a full sensory experience —sights, sounds, pain, and anguish. It showed me important things. And important things were almost always intense. I wasn't sure if I was ready to see Tina murdered.

I closed my eyes. Intention was everything with spell casting. If I went in scared, I would be setting myself up for failure. *Start with something easier, a warm-up spell to build my confidence.*

I flipped to the page that covered the spell for heightening my senses. I grinned. In the kitchen, I had a few cookies left over from my visit to Willy's. And I could use a few extra calories as a pick-me-up after all the magic I used at the college. My mouth watered as I scampered to the kitchen.

Only one cookie was left. Grace had apparently helped herself to the others this morning. I poured myself a glass of milk and prepped the area. I ran a finger over my sweater. While it wasn't something I would normally notice, the weave had a bumpy texture that could be scratchy once my sense of touch was amplified. I quickly changed into a silk blouse, lowered the blinds, and dimmed the lights in the kitchen.

I settled down on a stool and placed the journal on one side and the cookie and milk on the other. As I shook out my arms, I read through the spell one last time before muttering the words. I had used this spell enough times that I didn't need the book anymore. I remembered the words without it. As with the relaxation potion, as the words left my mouth, motes of light appeared in the air and spiraled around me. First, they settled into my hands before swirling upward around my face. My skin warmed, and the light filled my vision. I blinked. The light disappeared and was replaced with a soft glow around the edges of my vision.

Everything around me came into sharp focus. The silk against my skin was smooth and cool. Each individual sprinkle on the cookie stood out in stark relief against the white icing. I exhaled slowly and continued the incantation. Sense by sense, things returned to normal as I dampened the need for heightened vision, touch, and sound. I left the heightened sense of taste.

I picked up the peppermint spritz cookie, and the flavor exploded in my mouth as I bit into it. Normally, everything mingled into a single taste, but with the spell active, I could taste each part of the cookie separately: the dough, the icing, the peppermint sprinkles. It tasted amazing. I stifled a moan as I savored each bite.

The grandfather clock at the end of the hall chimed the hour. I took one last bite and dropped the spell. Grace could come home at any minute, and I still needed to practice the spell to activate the Sight.

I filled a bowl with water and carried it into the living room. I moved the easy chair from the corner and set it up in front of the fireplace so that I could see out into the driveway in case Grace came home halfway through.

Balancing the bowl in my lap, I held the journal over it and followed the directions in order, starting with filling the bowl with water. I dipped my finger into the water and drew a semicircle on my forehead. I sank into the chair and chanted the words to the spell. The first few times, I read straight from the journal, but after the fifth incantation, I could remember the words. Each repetition connected a sense to the past, with the final, sixth sense being that of the Sight.

As the last word left my lips, the room became dull and muted, as if I was seeing the room through a pane of water. It wasn't the same as it did when the Sight activated on its own.

Things shifted and undulated as I moved my head from side to side. I lowered my gaze and stared into the bowl. There, on the surface of the water, the image was crisper. It was morning. Sun streamed through the curtains. I shifted the bowl to see other parts of the room. The water sloshed, distorting the image for a moment before it settled.

Reflected in the water was Grace, sitting on the couch, her legs curled under herself. She looked up and stared straight at me, her eyes wide. My hands trembled. The water sloshed around the bowl, distorting the image. By the time the water settled, she was standing and walking out of view. I tried to follow her with the bowl, but she ducked into the hallway.

I stood and walked toward the hall. My leg caught on the edge of the coffee table, and I stumbled. The water spilled out onto the floor, breaking the spell.

"Shoot." I darted into the kitchen and grabbed a towel from under the sink.

I crouched and cleaned up the spilled water. *Was that from this morning? How was that important? I must have messed something up.*

By the time I'd wiped everything up, the exhaustion of casting two spells—especially with one new and complicated—back-to-back sank in. Magic was like a muscle, in a way. Using it tired me out. I needed to practice more before I could handle so much magic in one day.

I curled up on the couch with my laptop and checked my email. No new claims had come in. With a few hours to kill before dinner, I made a list of the things I knew versus the things I didn't know about the case. After noting twenty-odd things I didn't know, it became apparent this method was pointless. I deleted the list and started again with the pressing questions.

I needed to know more about the men Tina had in her life —who her stalker was and whom she'd met on the ferry. I needed to know who had the means, motive, and opportunity to murder her. Those questions were too big to answer in one session. *I need to start small. Let's focus on the knowns, her ex-boyfriend and her boss.*

Since I knew what he looked like, I pulled up the ex-boyfriend's social media and scrolled through his profile. Everything he'd said during our quick meeting was there. He lived in Mukilteo and attended the community college there. He worked at a bar nearby called the Twisted Squirrel. Most of his posts were sarcastic memes and posts about football.

Shaking my head, I closed his page and searched for the boss, Owen Gallagher. He wasn't hard to find. All his public posts were professional. I hovered over his information. He lived on Whidbey Island too. *Is he the guy from the ferry?* I couldn't tell how tall he was in the photos, but he was handsome with brown hair. *He would have to take it in, too, but then why would they only meet once a week?*

He was married. Maybe that had something to do with the secrecy. I clicked over to his wife's profile. She'd played basketball in college and played three years professionally before she retired. All her posts were too polished to be candid. With few exceptions, they were all about the community center in Langley. She hosted fundraisers for them and coached their basketball program.

Charlie flopped onto my lap, pushing the keyboard away with his paws. I chuckled and petted him while I continued to scroll. "I think you're right, buddy. There isn't anything useful here."

He rubbed his head against my hand, purring.

"I need someone to bounce ideas off of. You want to go hang out with Heather and Star for a bit?"

His head jerked up at the word *Star*. He leaped from the couch and sauntered over to where I kept his harness.

"I'll take that as a yes."

He wouldn't stop staring at me until I stood and got ready to go.

Charlie scampered ahead of me into the Bizzy Bean. Star, who'd been curled up at the top of cat castle, launched herself onto the ground. They ran toward each other, their tails held high behind them. Charlie tackled her, but she deftly flipped him onto his side and began cleaning his ears.

I scanned the room, searching for Heather. It was well after lunch, and the cafe was due to close its doors in a few minutes, at five. She sat squished between the Retirees at their usual table. I waved and wandered over.

The group was quiet as I approached. Heather sat perched on the edge of her seat, watching them with bated breath as they chewed. A plate full of cookies sat between them.

Betty reached for another cookie. "I think I'll need to try another one to be sure."

Agnes and Sarah followed suit.

"Should I take the third cookie as a good sign?" Heather gripped the edge of the table.

"Definitely." Agnes mumbled around her mouthful of cookie.

"What's this?" I asked, hovering over them.

"After you left the other day, I got inspired." Heather scooped up a cookie and handed it to me. "I experimented a little. I present to you my newest recipe: caramel apple pie sugar cookies."

"It's all the best things about the fall in one bite," Sarah said, licking her fingers clean.

The cookie was soft and warm. It was a brown sugar cookie that had been half hollowed out and filled with gooey apple pie filling, with caramel drizzled on top. I bit into the cookie. It was better than the peppermint spritz. "Oh, Heather, you really have outdone yourself this time. These need to go on your menu. And... in the gift baskets as well?"

"Of course! I've been—"

The bell over the front door chimed, and the mailman walked in. Heather surged to her feet and scuttled around the table toward him. "Anything from the health department?"

He handed her a bundle of mail. "I put it right there on top."

We all watched as she tore the envelope open. Her face fell. The mailman put a hand on her shoulder and backed out of the cafe. The Retirees shuffled back to their seats to give her space.

"That bad, huh?" I asked.

She chewed on her knuckle and furrowed her brow as she read.

I led her to the booth in the back. She slumped onto the bench as she read through the letter a second time.

"What's it say?"

She shook her head and slammed the letter down as the Retirees glanced over and continued their conversation in rushed tones. "I've lost my A-plus rating."

"Is that—"

"They want me to prove the cats aren't getting into the food-prep areas. Prove it? Couldn't they tell that during their inspection? We have a double-door system to get into the kitchen. A cat has never, not once, been back there."

I sat in stunned silence. Heather kept a cleaner kitchen than most restaurants. "And if you can prove that, you get your A-plus rating back?"

"Maybe?" She chewed on her fingernails. "If I can't, it says I can face fines. Or"—she leaned forward and lowered her voice—"be closed down. They've given me two weeks."

"What do you need?"

She reread the letter. "I don't even know where to begin. How do I prove that?"

"Why don't we try building a plexiglass wall? The cats stay on one side, the counter and the kitchen on the other?"

A small smile touched the corners of her mouth. "That could work. It would need a door."

"While I'm no Jessica, it should be a simple enough job that even my limited construction skills would suffice." I pulled out a notebook from my pocket and did a miniature sketch. "I was thinking something—"

A woman slid into the booth next to Heather.

She had bright-orange hair cut into a modern shag. Her bangs hung low over her forehead, covering part of her dark-brown eyes. I'd never seen her before in my life. Heather blinked at her, slack-jawed.

"This is a private conversation," I said.

"I'll only need a minute." Her voice was instantly recognizable. It was the reporter, the one who'd gotten me kicked off the fire scene but also given me the information that helped prove Clint's innocence.

I clenched my jaw. "Isabella Carter. So nice to put a name to a face."

She looked between me and Heather. Heather crossed her arms and leaned back in her seat, her eyebrows raised.

The reporter sighed and tugged at the hair. "It's Izzy. And… I should probably start this conversation by letting you know I'm not in charge of the story anymore. It was transferred to a more seasoned reporter." Bitterness crept into her voice as she said *seasoned*.

"Then why—"

"My best friend is Tina's sister. She was transferred to Spain last month. And their parents are somewhere in the Congo, volunteering for the Peace Corps. They can't do anything to push this investigation along from where they're at. So… that leaves me." She handed me her phone. "Hit Play."

It was a Snapchat video recording. Tina was sitting in her bedroom. She was clearly the one holding the camera. She had a wide smile on her face. I hit Play.

"Hey, sis. I don't have time for our usual call. But I just wanted to let you know that I've heard you. I know you've been worried about me." A pleased smile crossed her lips as she looked away, off camera. She fidgeted with a silver necklace of a stylized rose around her neck. "You don't have to, though. Everything is fine. It's more than fine, actually. Everything is great. I have some wonderful news to share. It's a secret for now, but soon. Very soon. I promise. So, relax, okay? I love you."

I replayed the video before handing back the phone. *Did this have something to do with the mystery man on the ferry? Or something else?* "Do you know what the news was?"

"I don't. But Becky received this the night Tina died. Whatever secret this was, I can't help but wonder if it got her killed."

"Why are you showing this to me?"

Izzy leaned into the table as she held my gaze. "While I might not be a seasoned journalist, I'm not an idiot. I know you've helped bring a murderer to justice before. Call me an optimist, but I'm hoping for a repeat performance."

I swallowed. *Do people really think of me as someone who solves murders? I've only solved one... and here I am, trying to solve another.*

"Have you shown this to the police?"

She scoffed. "They are so certain they have the right guy already I doubt they are looking anywhere else. I played it for the sheriff, and he thanked me for my time and sent me packing."

I blinked. *Are they still holding Clint?* I opened my mouth.

"I promise to tell you if I discover anything new. Can you do the same?" Izzy asked.

I nodded. *They have to. But why? He has an alibi.* My heart sank. They hadn't followed up on my tip because it came from me.

She reached into her pocket and slid a business card across the table. Without another word, she was up and out of the cafe. I picked up the card and read it: Isabella Carter—Entertainment Reporter for the *Island County Gazette*. She really was far away from her usual stories.

I showed Heather the card.

"Are you really going to call her if you find something?"

"I don't know…" I fidgeted with the card.

"Dani?"

"I… may have already found something."

I updated her on my investigation so far.

"Do you think her boss might be the mystery man?" she asked.

"The one from the ferry? Maybe. The question is, who is the stalker? Why was she being followed? And which mystery man left her house that night?"

"What are you going to do next?"

"I don't know yet." I had an idea, but it was half formed. If the Sight activation spell had worked, I would be off trying to cast it outside the house, but it had showed me only a few hours earlier, and not anything important, like it should have. I couldn't risk getting the cops called on me for loitering near a crime scene for nothing.

"Good luck." She squeezed my hand. "This day has turned into a mess, hasn't it?"

"It has."

"How's your business going?"

I slumped into the booth. Except for the fire loss, I hadn't received another claim since opening my doors. I couldn't help but wonder if all my business contacts were waiting to see how I handled this one before sending me something—one test case to secure my career.

"That bad, huh?"

"No new claims."

"That's probably because we haven't sent the gift baskets out yet. Once they go out, you'll have more business than you know what to do with."

"Thanks, Heather." I smiled. "Sorry I left during our last baking session. Are you still willing to help?"

"Of course. In fact, I have most of the cookies made already. Let's package them up together." She picked up the letter and slid out of the booth. "It'll help keep my mind off of my own impending doom."

CHAPTER 12

Heather and I had baked and packaged cookies late into the night. Midnight had come and gone before my head hit my pillow. When my alarm went off, I was tempted to throw it across the room. I dragged myself out of bed. Charlie had played with Star and the new kittens most of the evening, so he was too tired to come in with me. I left him dozing in bed with Grace when I headed into the office to mail out the packages.

The fall and winter were slow seasons on the island. With all the tourists gone for the year, downtown Point Pleasant was quiet. I drove through the deserted streets and parked right outside my office. Signs lined the roadway, advertising upcoming roadwork. While the winter wasn't the best weather for it, the reduced traffic made it the best time of year. The lights for the agency across the foyer were already on when I ducked inside.

I paused in the doorway and stared into my overflowing office. The last thing we'd done the night before was to haul all the gift baskets to my office. We piled them on every available surface. At least thirty packages of cookies had to be there, tastefully piled into baskets and wrapped with colorful paper and clear plastic, with large bows pinned to their tops. While I made several dozen cookies myself, Heather had done the bulk of the work.

I checked my email. My heart sank when I saw only one new message. It was from the property manager on the fire loss. *Still no new claims.* My eyes flicked between the screen and the gift baskets. I had to get them out in the mail, but I also had to get this fire claim wrapped up. If I could turn in a good work product, that would go a long way to getting more claims. But Heather was right—the gift baskets might also do the trick.

I opened the email. It was the lost rental-income paperwork. I quickly scanned through the documents. It was a fairly standard rental agreement. She had a year lease she'd agreed to in August. I blinked at the rent amount. She'd been paying three thousand dollars a month for the home. *How on earth can a college student afford that on her own?* I flipped to the check copies.

Owen Gallagher.

I blinked. I'd half expected her parents to have signed her rent checks, not her boss. I flipped through the four checks he'd signed. The first three were received on time, but the last check was one week late. *Were they having an affair? A week late... Does that mean they were having trouble in paradise?*

My head swiveled between the screen and the gift baskets. "Postage can wait."

I called the office where Owen worked and held my breath as the phone rang. Katie picked up on the third ring. "Financial aid. This is Katie."

"Hi, Katie. This is Dani. Will Owen be in today? I needed to chat with him quickly about Tina's wages," I lied.

Papers shuffled in the background. "He'll be in at ten."

"Sounds good. I'll call back then." I hung up.

Would he be honest over the phone? I tapped my nails against the table. *Probably not.* There was only one way to be sure he was being honest, and that was to interview him in person. I grabbed one of the gift baskets and headed for the docks.

I took the next ferry out to Mukilteo. Students crowded the streets as I drove across the campus to the parking garage. In the small window between classes, everyone was scrambling from one building to the next. I found a spot on the fourth floor of the garage then grabbed the gift basket from my passenger seat and took the elevator down. It opened in the section reserved for campus staff. Most of the spots were filled. I walked down the line, reading the names on the wall.

I found Owen's space halfway down the line. A red Ford Explorer was parked in his spot. My heart skipped a beat. Not only was Owen there, but he also drove a vehicle that matched the description Willy had given me during his interview of the car parked near Tina's house the night of the fire. I noted the license plate and scurried out of the garage. Weaving among students, I made my way to the student union building.

I took the winding staircase up two steps at a time and marched down the hall toward the financial aid office, rehearsing what I was going to say in my head as I walked. As I approached the door to the office, it swung outward, and a familiar shock of orange hair strode into the hall. I exchanged glances with Izzy, who stepped through the door as a group of students walked by. I pressed myself against the wall to let the group pass. Before I could get a word out, she darted into the crowd and disappeared down the stairs.

Shoot. If she's already questioned him, he might already be on edge. Should I come back another time? I was too late. My feet had already carried me into the office, and I stood facing Katie.

"Dani, I wasn't expecting to see you today. Is everything okay?"

"I realized I had business in town, so I figured I might as well drop by in person. Is Owen available?"

"He is." She stood and knocked on his door then ducked her head inside. "You're a popular guy today. You got enough time to talk to one more?"

His voice was too muffled to make out what he said. While Katie's back was turned, I whispered the words to the relaxation potion spell over the cookie basket. I'd used the spell a few times since discovering I was a witch, and it seemed to hold for only about twenty minutes. If he was in a talkative mood, that would be more than enough.

She backed out of the room. "He's got a few minutes. Go on in."

I rounded the counter and walked into his office, the cookies glowing under my arms. Thank goodness I was the only one who could see my magic.

Owen stood when I entered the room and gestured to the chair opposite him. He was a good half a head taller than me. He had a runner's body, slender but well muscled. He could fit Gwen or Willy's description. "What can I do for you today, Miss…?"

"Williams. Dani Williams." I set the gift basket down as I took a seat. "First, I wanted to extend my condolences for your loss. It's always tough losing an employee."

He eyed the cookies.

"Fresh baked. You should try the apple pie cookies. They are divine."

After a few seconds, he caved and reached out to unwrap the gift. He pulled out a cookie and politely set it next to himself.

"Thank you, but it wasn't necessary for you to stop by." He was forcing his body to appear relaxed by leaning back in his chair, but his shoulders were tense. He twisted a fraternity ring on his thumb as he spoke.

"I was on campus anyway. My daughter was thinking about coming here in the fall."

"That's nice." He twisted the ring again and reached out for the cookie. He broke off a corner and sniffed at it. "It's an excellent school. We have a lot of great direct-transfer options to four-year programs too."

"Good to know. I don't want to take up a lot of your time, but I'm investigating the fire." I studied him over the desk.

At the word *investigating*, he flinched, a small movement he quickly covered by biting the cookie.

"I'm a claims adjuster. And, well, while the police wrap up their investigation, I thought it would be best to cross all of my T's and dot all of my I's."

"Oh? And what can I do to help you?" He swallowed the piece of cookie and put the rest back down.

Please work. Please let one bite be enough. "Well, I was wondering who I would need to contact to request her wage information. Is that something you could help me with?"

"The work study department placed her here. While loosely connected to this office, it's overseen by a different administrator. Katie can get you their information."

I scanned the room. My excuse for being here was quickly running its course, and the spell hadn't taken hold yet. My gaze landed on the webcam above his desk, and I bit back a smile. If the relaxation spell wouldn't work, I could at least see the conversation he'd just had with the reporter. She'd promised to share, but I'd only recently met her. *Is she the type of person to keep promises?* I needed him to leave the room so I could work my magic on the camera.

"If there isn't anything else..." He stood.

My gaze landed on his full coffee cup. I surged upward to shake his hand. My palms became sweaty as I reached awkwardly across the table. I would only have one chance at this. "Thank you for your time." As my hand came back, I hit the coffee cup, spilling the cup all over the desk.

He leaped back as the coffee splashed out onto his lap.

"Oh my gosh. I am so sorry."

He stared in horror at his coffee-covered desk.

"Do you have paper towels?" I asked sweetly.

He blinked. "In the break room." He darted around his desk to collect them.

The door swung shut behind him, leaving me alone. I reached into my bag to get out my gran's journal. My fingers closed around nothing. I groped around inside, but my fingers kept closing on empty air. I pulled it all the way open. The journal was gone. *Did I take it out at home?* I tried to always put it back, but I must've left it out the last time I used it.

I spun in the office, cursing under my breath. That spell wasn't one I'd practiced enough, and I didn't remember the words to the memory-recall spell. With only seconds of being alone in the office, I opened his drawers. Nothing popped out as important.

I glanced into the trash and noticed a bundle of receipts. I grabbed them and shoved them into my purse as he walked back into the room. He blinked at me standing behind his desk, so I quickly grabbed a few things and set them aside, out of the reach of the spreading coffee.

"Good thinking." He tore off a large section of towel and handed me the rest of the roll. I followed suit and helped wipe up the mess. I tossed the soaking towels into the trash can, where the bundles of receipts had been moments before.

Once the desk was cleaned off, he sank back into his chair and grabbed the rest of the cookie from the corner of his desk. He popped it into his mouth and chewed. The warm glow of the spell seeped into his skin.

"Was there something else you needed?" he asked.

"I had a question about her—"

The office door swung open, and a tall and imposing woman marched into the room. She towered over both of us, her wide shoulders well muscled from her years of playing basketball. Emily Gallagher was a powerful presence in the room. Her features were striking and her eyes a brilliant green. Owen bolted upright in his chair and wiped the cookie crumbs from his fingers.

"Who's this?" Her words came out clipped.

I swallowed and stood. "Dani Williams. Insurance adjuster. I'm working on the fire claim at Tina's house… one of the employees who worked here."

Emily glanced between me, the gift basket, and her husband. "Owen is on a diet." She grabbed the package and thrust it toward me. "Perhaps you should give these to someone else." She turned to her husband. "You were supposed to meet me for breakfast."

My hands closed around the basket. My vision tunneled in on the basket until everything else was blurry. Adrenaline surged through me, and my heart pounded in my ears. Rage. The intensity of the emotion threw me off balance.

"I'm sorry, darling, I forgot to put it in my planner."

I blinked and forced a smile onto my face. "I always loved breakfast dates. Were you guys going somewhere fun?"

Emily frowned. "It's a quiet diner around the corner. To make relationships work"—she glared at him—"you have to make the time. Right, dear?"

He nodded, his face flushed.

"Then we should be going." She marched out the door.

Owen shrugged at me and followed her out. I lingered for a second longer before following. By the time I got to the stairs, they were disappearing out the front door. I took my time exiting the building.

That whole interaction was odd. The amount of hatred and rage that came off his wife was alarming. *We only just met. Why did she hate me so much? Was it me? Or was it me being alone with her husband? Or was she mad at him?*

As I stepped outside, the first raindrop fell on my head. It was cold as it slid down my nose, making my nose twitch. I pulled my coat as tight around me as I could with one hand. The bundle of cookies got in the way, catching the corner of the collar.

Another raindrop hit my head, followed by a downpour. Water slid down my neck and into my coat. I ran for the closest building and ducked inside to wait out the storm. I peered out. The rain pounded against the windows, obscuring my vision of the sidewalk beyond.

I retreated farther into the building. It was an addition built in the sixties. The vinyl flooring was worn and a little dingy around the corners. I stopped at a row of benches and took a seat.

Across the way was a floor-to-ceiling bulletin board. Half of it was filled with various openings for psychological tests, while the rest was a hodgepodge of want ads for roommates or events on campus, with no rhyme or reason to the organization. The board was covered by one post after another, the older ones half buried behind the new additions. Tucked into a corner was a post with a familiar face on it.

I stood and moved a #throwbackthursday potluck advertisement to the side, revealing a list of guest lecturers with the key speakers' photos together at the top. In the middle of the grouping was Brad Parsons, the fire investigator. I shivered as a tingle ran down my spine. *Was that the cold or my Sight?*

The rain outside came to a sudden stop. My head jerked toward the door. Downpours in the Seattle region were sporadic and hard to predict. Frequently, we would get only a temporary reprieve before the rain picked back up. In case it was my Sight, I grabbed the guest-lecturer list off the wall, shoved it into my purse, and sprinted out of the building.

I made it most of the way to my car before the rain picked up again. Running the last few feet to the garage, I gasped for air, my breath ragged. Over the past few months, I'd worked almost exclusively from my living room. What little stamina I had for running was gone. I shuffled to my car and turned the heater on full blast.

While I waited for the car to warm up, I pawed through the scraps of paper I'd shoved into my purse. It was a mess. I sorted through them, pulling out my own receipts so that they wouldn't get mixed in with Owen's trash. That was easy enough since all my receipts were for things like coffee or fare for the boat. All of his, on the other hand, were gambling receipts.

I put the gambling receipts in order and flipped through them. They went back only a few days, but if they were any indication of his habits, Owen was deep in a hole. *Is this why he'd been late paying her rent? If he is the guy from the boat and she was his mistress, had she threatened to tell his wife if he didn't get his gambling under control?* I bit my lip. That was a wild theory, but it would explain Emily's reaction.

I was deciding between marching back into the school and asking Katie about it and springing the news on Samuel. He'd seemed bitter when I spoke to him. *Maybe he knew about the affair.* I pulled out my phone and checked the hours for the Twisted Squirrel. It was a Friday night, which is always a bar's busiest. He would be there when it opened. *Eight hours until the doors open.* The image of the gift baskets came to mind.

I drove the long way back to Point Pleasant. The entire drive, I flip-flopped between mulling over the case and trying to decide who to send the goody bags to. That night, I would know more, but for the moment, I had to be satisfied with being productive on another front. The gift baskets wouldn't mail themselves out.

After a long day of boxing up gift baskets and mailing them out, I was exhausted. I fought back a yawn as I pulled into a parking spot a block away from the Twisted Squirrel. It was a quarter past six. The sun had set over an hour before. I'd driven past the bar at first and had to double back. Its front door was in an alleyway behind a coffee shop. The door was thick and had one of those old-timey door panels that slid open for someone to give a passphrase to get in. It felt very 1920s speakeasy.

I hovered outside the door. *Do I need to knock or just go in?* I tried the handle. It wasn't locked. Inside was a long, narrow room. No tables were there, only two bars running the length of the walls, with stools bolted to the floor below them. At the far end of the bar was a tiny stage illuminated by a spotlight overhead. The whole place felt cramped, with an air of excitement simmering below the surface.

It had been open for about seventeen minutes, and the bar was already filling up. About a dozen patrons were perched on stools or standing in small groups along the narrow walkway. I swallowed, straightened my shoulders, and approached the counter with as much confidence as I could muster.

The bartender was halfway down the counter, serving a group of college students. I tapped the bar to get his attention and caught his eye. He nodded and finished up their order before sashaying toward me. He wore a trim teal suit with a navy cravat. Tattoos poked around the corners of his sleeves and collar.

"What can I get for you, sweetheart?" he purred.

"I was hoping to speak with Sam. Do you know when he'll be in?"

"Sam who?"

"Koenig. He works here."

He pursed his lips. "I don't think so."

"Are you sure?" I leaned against the counter.

"Positive. I'm the owner. I know all of my employees' names, and not one of them is called Sam."

I pulled out my phone and showed him a picture. "So this man doesn't work here?" *Did I write down the wrong place?*

He studied the picture. "He doesn't have the right look. We're more vintage, but whimsical." The bar door opened, and a group of six more customers sauntered in. "We have a show starting in fifteen. I really got to get all these orders taken before Mrs. Robinson goes on. You sure you didn't want something? She puts on a fantastic show."

I shook my head and backed away from the bar. The newcomers filled the area, crowding in around the bar to put in their orders. I took one last glance around the space. While a lot of fun, it did not strike me as a place a sports jock would frequent.

The cool air bit into my skin as I left the bar. I retreated to my car and huddled in front of the air vents until the engine warmed up. I rechecked Koenig's profile to make sure I hadn't taken down the wrong establishment. His profile clearly said Twisted Squirrel. It was a unique name. I couldn't find another one anywhere in Washington. *Why would he lie about where he works? If he wasn't at work when Tina died, then where was he? What else is he hiding?*

I stared blankly at my phone, stuck in an unexpected dead end. The questions and suspects were multiplying faster than answers. I needed backup. *Chris?* I slumped forward in my seat and rested my head against my steering wheel. *He'll warn me off again. Izzy? If she was serious about sharing info, maybe she has a thread I can pull.* I took out the reporter's business card and punched in her number.

"Did you find something?" Izzy whispered into her phone. She was hard to hear over the music in the background.

"I was calling to ask you the same thing," I stuttered.

Her heels clicked against tile flooring, then a door closed, cutting off the noise. "It's complicated. I don't have time to talk right now."

"When should I call back?"

"I think this conversation would be better in person."

"Why don't you come by my office?"

"I'll be there. Bright and early. Eight a.m. tomorrow morning." She hung up before I could respond.

CHAPTER 13

I jerked awake to the sound of my alarm clock. The room was dark. That late in the year, even with the accursed Daylight Savings Time, the sun didn't rise until almost seven thirty. I blinked at my alarm clock. It read 6:03 a.m. Grace had been home the whole previous day, so I hadn't been able to search for the misplaced journal yet. I groaned and climbed out of bed. I wasn't ready to answer questions about why the journal was important yet, and Grace had the same curiosity gene I did. If I asked her about it, she would want to know what it was. I had to look for it while she was asleep.

My search started in the bedroom then branched out to the home office, the living room, the dining room, and the darkroom I'd created in the basement. It wasn't in any of those places. I tore the couch apart and shifted every piece of furniture I could think of, to no avail. I hadn't been in the other rooms of the house since I used the book last, but in desperation, I checked them as well.

Time was ticking by, quickly approaching when I'd have to leave to make it into the office for my meeting, and I hadn't found the book. It was my main connection to my gran. It had her words in it. Misplacing it felt like I'd betrayed her memory somehow.

I peeked into Grace's room. She sprawled across the bed, fast asleep, her arm thrown across her pile of pillows. *Why am I looking in here? I wouldn't have taken it here... and Grace is a good girl.*

I backed out of the room and tiptoed back to the entrance hall. *The car, maybe?* I slipped my shoes on and grabbed my purse. Charlie appeared at my side and wound his way around my legs, purring.

"Did you want to come too?" I whispered.

He chirped in response.

I grabbed his harness, hooked him to his leash, and shuffled to the car. He sat perched on the dashboard while I searched every inch of my car. I moved the seats around and checked under them with a flashlight. I pulled out my home inspection kit and unpacked and repacked it. The journal was nowhere to be found.

The sun crept up over the horizon. I put the kit back in the trunk and slumped into the driver's seat. "Maybe I left it at the office."

Charlie cocked his head and took his place in the passenger seat.

Traffic was light as I headed into the office. I arrived with fifteen minutes to spare. I parked and dashed inside. My heart beat quickly in my chest as I searched my office. I found a misplaced pocket notebook, three cat toys, and a roll of tape, but no journal.

I paced the room. Izzy was due any minute. *Where is it? What happens if I can't find it? Am I going to be continuing my journey into becoming a witch blind?*

I called Betty. She'd hinted to me on more than one occasion she knew my gran's secret, but we'd never outright talked about it. She always pushed off the conversation and said now was not the time to discuss such things, without acknowledging what "such things" were. The call went to voicemail.

"Hey, Betty. This is Dani. I know we haven't had a serious talk about my gran yet. We should have by now. It's just…" I faltered. *Just what? I feared what other secrets she may have been keeping? Is that why I never pushed for her to open up?* "I need your help. I can't find her journal, and I don't know what to do."

Izzy knocked on the office door. I dropped my phone on my desk and scurried to the door to let her in. Charlie trotted over and sniffed at her.

"I love what you've done with the place." She kneeled down next to Charlie and held out a hand for his inspection.

"This is Charlie. He's the unofficial office mascot." I closed the door behind her. "Can I get you something to drink?"

"No, thanks. I've already had three coffees this morning." She scratched Charlie under his chin and stood. "How did your meeting with Owen go yesterday?"

"Not well." I took a seat. "He was cagey at first. By the time I got him to relax, our meeting got cut short by his wife. Was yours more productive?"

"Not really."

"What were you there to talk to him about?"

"I got my hands on Tina's phone records."

My heart skipped a beat, and the tingling at the back of my mind returned. *This is important.* I inched forward and locked eyes with her. "What did you find?"

She looked down and picked at her fingernails. "I'm not sure yet. I found some unusual activity. For the past six months, she would call the same number, and like twenty minutes later would get a text back saying it was done. She didn't save this number on her phone. When I dug into it, I couldn't find any records of who owns it. I think it's a prepaid burner phone. Last month—"

We jumped as my phone rang. I lunged for it and turned it to silent. "Sorry about that. You were saying?"

"Last month, she called that number four times over about a week, with no responding text. She then called her boss, Owen, and twenty minutes later, she got the same text from the unknown number, saying it was done. Except this time, it came with a second message."

"A second message? What did it say?"

"'This is the last time. If you were going to do something, you would have already.'"

"Wow." I sat back, stunned. *Was she blackmailing someone?*

"That's not all." She inched forward in her seat. "She called that number again the night she died."

I slid forward and perched on the edge of my seat.

"Six times. And afterward, she called Owen twice. The second time, the call lasted almost seven minutes. This time, she didn't get any texts back."

"Do you think he owns that number?"

"I don't know. But it sure seems like it. And when I asked him if he had spoken to Tina the day she died, he initially denied it and then tried to brush it off as a conversation about approving a time-off request. But according to her calendar, she doesn't have any plans to go out of town until winter break. The college is closed during winter break. She wouldn't need time off for that."

I gripped the edge of my seat. The rent checks lingered in my mind. *Should I tell her? If I do, she might bring it straight to Owen and rush it like she rushed the phone records.* I clenched my jaw. *I don't know she did that. Am I being too hard on her?*

I fought with myself for a few seconds before I cracked and shared something. "Do you know anything about Sam?"

"They dated for a while, right?"

"Yeah. I've been looking into him."

"I hadn't really considered him. Tina barely mentioned

him, so Becky thought they weren't serious. He seemed so…normal when I talked to him."

"I thought so too. I had some follow-up questions for him, but when I stopped by where he claims to work, he doesn't work there. And never has."

"Huh." She leaned back, slack-jawed. "Well, that's a new thread to pull on."

"I thought so too. You'll tell me if you find something?"

Izzy nodded and stood. I promised I would call her if I found anything else and locked up behind her.

Tina seemed to be involved in questionable activities. *What was she to Owen? Mistress? Blackmailer? Or both?*

I picked up my phone to see who'd called during the meeting. I found six missed calls from Betty and a single text: "Call me!"

She answered before the phone finished its first ring. "Where have you been?"

"In a meet—"

"You left *that* on my voicemail and then went to a meeting? Are you trying to give this old girl a heart attack?"

"I'm sor—"

"Meet me at Slice of Life in five minutes."

The line went dead in my hands. I stared at it in disbelief. She'd hung up. Shaking my head, I grabbed my purse and headed out.

I rushed to the Slice of Life diner as quickly as my legs would carry me. It was half a block off the main drag, on a one-way street, which made it faster to walk than drive. I made it there in just under five minutes. I burst through the front doors, gasping for breath.

Willow stood behind the counter, her strawberry-blond hair piled on top of her head in a messy bun. She wore large yellow-framed glasses that made her wide-eyed expression almost comical. I giggled and bent over as the stitch that had been building in my side hit full steam. I raised my arm over my head and shuffled, half bent and giggling, into the restaurant.

"Are you okay?" Willow came around the counter and hovered over me.

"I'm meeting Betty. Didn't want to be late." I wheezed and straightened. The pain in my side twinged as I stretched it out. "Is she here?"

"She's at the table by the kitchen."

I straightened the rest of the way, smoothed down my hair, and forced a serious expression onto my face. I found Betty at the rear table. She wore her usual tracksuit. Her hair was in tight curls around her head. She picked at them as I approached, trying to break them up into her usual big-wave look. I slid into the booth across from her, and she attempted to glare at me, but it melted as she met my gaze.

She gripped my hand. "Tell me everything."

"There isn't much to tell. I can't find it. I must have misplaced it somewhere."

"Misplaced it? Where have you looked? When did you use it last? Has anyone else seen it?" Her words tumbled over each other in their haste to get out.

"Everywhere. I mean, everywhere I could think of. Almost every room in the house. My car. The office. I only keep it in two places, and it isn't in either. But with Grace being home, the house has been a bit more disorganized than usual. Is there a spell that can find it?" I swallowed.

Betty didn't blink at the word *spell*. She furrowed her brow and pursed her lips. "There is one. I can write it down for you."

I handed her my notebook. She hunched over it and wrote almost three full pages in her wide, looping cursive script. She slid it toward me across the table.

Halfway through reading the first page, my heart started to race. The spell was more complicated than any I'd attempted to date. I peered up at her. "If you know the spell, are you capable of casting it?" I held my breath.

"I can't."

"Does that mean you're not a—"

"I am one. I can't cast this."

"Did my gran know?"

"When we were younger, we were in a coven together."

My mind reeled. *A coven? Why didn't I think of that before?* I sat back in my chair and stared at her. "If you are one, and you know the spell, then why can't you? It's complicated. Far more complicated than anything I've cast to date."

"It is complicated. And that's why you don't want me to cast it. Too many places for things to go wrong."

I sat there, stunned. *How do I ask my next question without sounding rude?* I opened and closed my mouth three times before I could force the question out. "Are you bad at magic?"

She slid forward in her seat and studied my eyes. "You don't know about the curse, do you?"

"What curse?"

She closed her eyes, shaking her head. "Your gran did you a big disservice. She never mentioned the curse? Not once in the entire journal?"

"She said our family was ill-fated. Is that what you mean?"

"Yes. In a manner of speaking." She rubbed at the bridge of her nose. "It's too complicated to get into right now. But once you've got the journal back, I promise you, we will sit down together, and I'll give the whole story. In very broad strokes, something happened when we were much, much younger, which cursed our families. Every family involved has something they are innately good at, and this curse twisted it. Your ability to see, your Sight—capital-*S* Sight— became volatile and dangerous for you, especially when it begins to manifest for the first time. Before, it only came when you called for it. But now... there were entire weeks where your gran couldn't take off her gloves."

She curled in on herself. Betty, who'd always been so feisty, was small and gave off the air of someone who'd been defeated. I put my hand over hers. "What happened to your family?"

"Ours was the family of change. It made it so every spell we cast has unintended changes. The more complicated the spell, the bigger the consequences. It made it so we became afraid to cast, afraid of what horrible things might happen because we used magic." A single tear slid down her cheek. She wiped it away, sniffing. "I don't cast anymore. Not if I can help it."

A cold weight settled into my stomach. I sat with my mouth open, shaking my head. "How? Why? What happened? Did someone curse us? Did we do something to deserve it?"

"When you have the journal, I'll tell you everything. But you have to find it first. It's important that it doesn't fall into the wrong hands."

"Are there evil witches out there? Am I in danger?"

She patted my hand. "You're going to be okay. Practice with small things first. Like your keys."

"Can anyone cast spells if they find it?"

"No, you have to be a witch already. And while it's technically not against the rules, the Council frowns on knowledge like this getting out. But they won't punish you for it."

"Council? What?" I gulped. My heart skipped a beat.

"So long as you don't violate the Rules of Magic, you'll be fine."

"What rules?" I blurted, my voice coming out louder than intended.

Betty leaned in and lowered her voice. "She really didn't tell you anything, did she?"

I shook my head. *Why did no one tell me? It should have been in the letter.* My pulse quickened, and my vision tunneled in on Betty's face. *Why didn't she tell me?*

"It's easy enough. There are only three of them. You're a

good person, Dani. These are the sorts of things you would feel wrong doing."

"What are they?" I asked through gritted teeth.

"You will not permanently alter another's mind, body, or spirit without their informed consent." She ticked off her fingers as she spoke. "You will not violate the natural order of things. And you will not make deals with Outsiders to augment your power."

"What does that even mean?"

Betty closed her eyes. "One step at a time. Journal and then story time."

"What happens if the rules are broken?"

"Bad things. They are rules for a reason. Don't break them, and you'll be fine."

"Didn't my—" I slammed my mouth closed before I could finish the question. *Didn't my gran break one when she suppressed my powers? Was my gran a bad witch?*

Betty squeezed my hand. "I will explain everything. You have my word. But that is a very large and complicated conversation that will derail the important things. And right now, the important thing is for you to find the journal."

I nodded.

After a few more minutes, she got up and left. I reread through the spell but couldn't focus on the words. My mind was reeling. Only a few months had passed since I found out I was a witch. Now, I was not just a witch—I was a cursed witch, fumbling through a paranormal society I didn't understand.

I swallowed. *How on earth am I supposed to learn all of this? It's too much, Gran. Why didn't you prepare me?* I choked back a sob and refocused on the words. *One step at a time. Keys. Journal. And then answers.*

CHAPTER 14

I walked back to my office in a daze and picked Charlie up. He gazed at me with his bright-blue eyes the entire ride home. When I pulled into the driveway, Grace's car was gone again. I sat, the engine slowly cooling, and stared blankly up at the house. Charlie inched forward in his seat and placed a single paw on my hand.

"It's okay, buddy. I've got a lot on my mind." I scratched under his chin, and he purred.

I shivered. The car had become cold. I collected Charlie, and we shambled inside. I took a quick walk through the house. Grace really was out for the day.

The spell was a complicated one. I scratched my head as I reread the directions a third time. Half of the directions involved forging a connection to the object or person in question, which was easiest if the caster had a piece of what she was looking for. Betty had described it as a sympathetic connection. The closer or stronger the connection, the easier finding what you were searching for would be.

I grabbed my notebook and tore out a page. At the top of the page, I drew a waving stick figure, and at the bottom of the page, I drew an identical stick figure. When I took the time, I was a decent artist, but I was going for something simple and easy to replicate. I ripped the page in two and crumpled one half and threw it into the living room with Charlie.

I retreated into the hallway and listened. Charlie scampered back and forth across the room, batting the piece of paper around. Knowing Charlie, he would have it stuck behind a piece of furniture in no time. I wandered into the kitchen and made myself a cup of coffee. With all the running around I'd done that morning, I hadn't stopped for my first cup yet. As it percolated, I read through the spell again.

After a few minutes, I peeked into the hallway. The living room was silent. I grabbed the bag of cat treats and shook the bag. Charlie sprinted out of the living room and slid to a stop in front of me. I dropped a treat onto the floor in front of him and stashed the treats on the counter. He quirked his head to one side and looked between me and the single treat. Normally, I gave him three or four at a time. Each treat was barely a mouthful. He daintily picked it up and followed me back to the living room.

I poked my head around the corner and scanned the floor. The piece of paper was nowhere to be seen. A smile spread across my lips. I pulled the spell back out and held it in one hand, the other half of the notebook page in the other.

"I've got this." I whispered and began the spell. *Step one. I need to find the other half.*

Every time I cast a spell for the first time, it was a strange experience. The words felt off in my mouth, like the act of speaking them gave them flavor. The experience wasn't unpleasant but simply odd. I couldn't explain the flavor. It didn't taste like any food I'd ever eaten. It simply was.

Light flowed out of my mouth and spun around the room. I continued whispering the words, and the light formed a path for me. My eyes flicked between the motes of light and the cursive script. I missed the right line and started a section a second time. The lights in the room flashed, and the room went dark.

"Shoot." I scrambled for the light switch and flipped it off and back on. It flickered back to life on the second attempt.

Charlie jumped up on the couch and curled up next to the arm. He rested his chin on the armrest and stared at me.

"I know, buddy. That didn't go as planned. But I've got to try again."

He chirped and slowly blinked.

I went back to the hallway and began again. Upon a second attempt, the spell felt more familiar. I kept my eyes locked on the cursive script and blocked out the motes of light dancing in the air around me until I whispered the last word. I folded the spell and slid it into my pocket. In front of me was a shimmering path. I stepped into it and followed it into the living room.

Behind me, the trail had disappeared. I experimented with stepping off the path, but it followed me. The light trail went straight from me to the pile of wood next to the fireplace. I crept toward it. While the one end followed me wherever I went, the destination end stayed the same.

I kneeled in front of the firewood. The trail disappeared inside the wood. I reached into the pile and gingerly felt around. My fingers closed around a scrap of paper, and I pulled it out. The light trail moved to it. The paper glowed in my hand. I exhaled, releasing the spell.

"Did I do it, Charlie?" I unwrapped the scrap of paper and grinned. It was the silly stick figure I'd drawn. "Bingo."

I stood and dusted my pants off. *Now, I need to duplicate it.* I retreated to the kitchen and grabbed one of Charlie's cat toys from his basket. I plopped down at the kitchen island and drew the cat toy. I ate while I drew, to replenish my strength.

Convincing Charlie to play with his toy and repeat the

performance didn't take much. I needed three attempts to find the cat toy and two to find my keys. I slumped on the couch. My energy was waning. I grabbed another coffee and closed my eyes.

The day was still young, and Grace hadn't come home yet. *I have more of a connection to the book than the keys. This should work, right?* I retrieved a sketchbook from my closet and took my time drawing a replica of the journal. I'd spent many hours poring over its pages, so picturing its scratched leather cover and dented spine was easy.

I drew for almost an hour. I sipped cup after cup of coffee, refilling my reserves as I worked. My hand cramped. I sat back and stared at my handiwork. After two semesters of art in college, I wasn't half bad.

I held the drawing in one hand and the spell in the other. Inhaling deeply, I focused my will. *I need to find my grandmother's journal.*

The words of the spell poured out of me into motes of light. The room became brighter and brighter as the space filled with magic. *Lead me to the book.* The lights swirled and formed into a path as the last word left my mouth. I inched off the stool and followed the trail out of the kitchen and down the hall.

The trail went all the way up the stairs and disappeared under the door to the attic stairwell. I cocked my head to the side. *I didn't bring it up there.* Shaking my head, I followed the trail anyway. *Lead me to my grandmother's journal. The book she left me. My birthright.*

In the attic, the trail of light stopped in the middle of the room. I paced around the space, but no matter which angle I came at it from, it stopped at the same place. I stepped forward over to where the light disappeared. The floorboards creaked under my feet. *What on earth...?* I kneeled and felt around on the floor. My nails caught on the edge of a raised floorboard.

I blinked and shook my head. *How did it get here?* I worked my fingernails into the small gap between the floorboards and lifted. The board came up easily in my hand. Underneath, peeking out at me from between the slats, was a leather journal.

Over the past few months, I'd become more in tune with my abilities, so as my fingers brushed the cover, I knew instinctively that I'd never touched this book before. My breath bottled up in my chest. My limbs became light, as if I was floating.

I exhaled, and my heart skipped a beat as I pulled the journal out. I flipped it open, and a note fluttered out to the floor.

> *My dearest Dani,*
>
> *I know things have been confusing and scary for you. But know, my little bird, that I am so proud of you for taking the next steps on your journey. Know that I love you completely and entirely, with a full heart.*
>
> *If my guess is correct, you should have been dreaming about this journal for weeks. Dreams are funny that way. Now that you have found the second book, I have another confession. You are not alone.*
>
> *I felt almost cruel, keeping it from you when I wrote my first letter. Unfortunately, our family bears a unique weight no one else can fully understand. I thought, perhaps naively so, that learning to carry that weight without stopping to compare your journey with anyone else's would be good for you. But there I am again, aren't I? Making decisions about what is best for you without your input.*

I clenched my teeth as I reread the last sentence. I'd been carrying a weight around since finding out I was a witch. It wasn't anger, but it was close—a frustration so deep that it had settled into my core. I didn't want to admit it to myself, but the feeling of betrayal lingered in the back of my mind. That letter didn't alleviate the frustration. It poked at it, reminding me it was there. It reminded me that my gran had more secrets left to uncover—like the curse and the Council. Her best intentions had not kept me safe.

I stood and paced the room.

I loved my gran with all my heart. If only she were there so that I could shake some sense into her...

I digress. You are not alone. When I was much younger, I belonged to a coven of witches in our town. Most of them are still around and can help you in your next steps forward. I have tasked my most trusted friend to keep an eye out on you. When you find this, she will know, and she will reach out to you. Do not be startled. Embrace her words of wisdom.

I love you. And I hope, since you have found this book, it means you are well and may have space in your heart to forgive me for my follies.

Be well.

Gran

I wiped a tear from my cheek. In her last days, Gran had spent her time worrying about me instead of taking care of herself. As frustrated as I was, that truth had also settled into my heart. Love was complicated.

I'd probably jumped the gun on meeting the trusted friend. Gran hadn't anticipated me being choked out by a killer or losing the journal.

I flipped from page to page, taking in the new array of spells. Just like in the first book, each section contained page upon page of theory and explanation. Knowing a spell wasn't enough. She wanted me to know the how and why of it and the importance of the caster's intentions. I grinned when I stumbled across the locator spell I'd used to find this book.

For a moment, I considered using the same spell to find

all the other books, but that thought was caught short when I read the next paragraph. The locator spell couldn't be used to locate warded objects, and the remaining books were warded. *What is a ward? Some sort of protective spell?*

After the locator spell was an entire section on glamor spells that could make the caster or others appear different to the mind's eye.

Grace's car pulled into the driveway.

I stood and peeked out the attic window. Water slid down the pane as it drizzled outside. Grace sprinted from the car to the front door. I darted down the stairs to my room and stowed the book under my mattress.

Grace popped her head into my room as I straightened the blankets.

"Hey, Mom. You working from home today?"

I smoothed my hair back into place. "Yeah. You have fun exploring?"

She came in and flopped on my bed. "Does it get any less gray around here?"

I laughed. "Not between November and March. You gotta wait for March, and then it's the first spring."

"First spring?" She rose up on her elbows.

"It's a local joke. The weather around here can't make a decision. First winter, fake fall." I studied her. "If you stay, you'll get used to it."

She flopped back down and let out an extended, overly dramatic sigh. "I don't know if I could ever get used to that."

I perched on the edge of the bed. "Hey, honey, have you seen a journal lying around?"

"No."

"It's leather and belonged—"

"I'm tired." She sat up and surged off the bed. She bolted out of the room before I could get another word out.

I stared at the empty doorway. Grace was hiding something from me. *Did she find it? She would tell me, wouldn't she?* I chewed on the inside of my lip. *Friends always know what's going on.*

I pulled out my phone and rechecked her social media. She was friends with the same kids from high school. Her friend Madison had spent almost as much time at our house as she did her own throughout their senior year. My finger hovered over the message button. *I have to know.*

I typed a quick message. "Hey, Maddy! I wanted to get a jump start on Christmas shopping, and I have been wracking my brain for the last few days, to no avail. You got any fun ideas for what I should get Grace?" I hit Send. That was innocuous enough to start a conversation. If something else was wrong, I had to know before I accused her of taking something that didn't belong to her.

I flopped onto the bed. *Now what?* With Grace headed back to bed, I had more time to read. I fished the second journal back out from under the mattress and flipped it open to the first page.

CHAPTER 15

At four in the morning, Point Pleasant was a ghost town. Heather had texted me the night before to let me know the plexiglass had been delivered for the enclosure I'd promised to help her build. We hoped to get it built before her doors were scheduled to open at seven. The plexiglass panels, wrapped in honeycomb paper, rested against the far wall. Within minutes of stepping through the door, we were hard at work, cutting and nailing the wooden frames together.

"How is the case coming along?" Heather grunted as she tightened a clamp.

I filled her in on everything that had happened since we last spoke. The investigation had become more muddled.

"So you have two different mystery men, a lying ex-boyfriend with no alibi, a boss who she may or may not have been blackmailing, and his very tall and jealous wife?" She ticked them off on her fingers.

The suspect pool had expanded to five people. I exhaled sharply. "That sounds about right. It feels like every time I turn another stone over, I find more suspects. The only one I've been able to take off the list is Clint, and he's the one the sheriff still has in custody."

"What are you going to do next?"

I climbed a step stool to attach the first half of the frame to a stud in the ceiling. "Not sure. I don't even know where to start with the mystery men."

"So why not start with the ones you know? The first on the list was the ex-boyfriend. I think the question there is, Who is he really? If he lied about where he works, is he lying about something else? Is anything on his social media profile real?"

I peeked at her from under my arm. "What do you mean?"

"Catfishing. It may all be a lure to get something from Tina."

I blinked. I hadn't thought about that.

"I mean, think about it. She lived in an expensive house. She was young and, the assumption might be, foolish."

"If it was a catfish, then why is he still around? Wouldn't he have moved on by now?"

She furrowed her brow. "You're right."

After the frame was up and in place, we unwrapped the plexiglass and slid it into place. Heather stepped back and stared at it. Her eyes flicked between her custom-painted window display and the glass enclosure. "I should get this painted too."

I grinned. I could see it already, a wrap-around display. I imagined it feeling like sitting inside a snow globe. "I think you're right."

Something stuck in my mind about the idea of his profile being fake. *Was the lie for her or for someone else?* I couldn't get the idea out of my head as we attached the next section to the wall and slid the next piece of plexiglass into place.

When we stopped for a break, I took out my laptop and pulled up his social media profiles. I found him on three different sites. I pored through the posts and About Me sections. Not until I scrolled through everything a second time did I notice it. I opened each profile side by side and verified. I wasn't mistaken. He'd made all three of his profiles on the same day, seven months prior.

My heart raced in my chest as I grabbed one of his profile pictures that showed his face straight on and dropped it into Google to do a reverse image search. The first few pages took me straight back to his social media profiles. Buried deep on the seventh page, it took me someplace else.

I stared down at the face of a smiling Samuel Koenig except, according to the website, his name was Jacob Bryant, a forensic accountant. It was an old website. The accounting firm had been bought a year before. When I tracked the other former employees to their LinkedIn profiles, over half ended up working for the IRS. Jacob's led nowhere. His didn't exist. With that one exception, nothing mentioned a Jacob Bryant matching his description anywhere on the web.

I leaned back, stunned. "He might be a forensic accountant."

"What do forensic accountants do?"

"Investigate fraud."

Heather peered over my shoulder. "And you said Tina was blackmailing her boss?"

"I don't know for sure."

"What are you going to do now?" Heather asked.

I fidgeted, fighting the urge to dash off. If he was a forensic accountant, he probably knew more than he was letting on. *But why would he tell me anything?* I pulled out my phone and froze. The sun wasn't out yet, making it much too early to call. I texted him, starting the message with "Hi, Jacob," and asking for a meeting instead.

I glanced at the plexiglass wall. We'd fully encased the first two panels but had two more left to install.

"We can finish it later if you've got somewhere you need to be."

"I usually meet Chris on Tuesday mornings. He gets stuck with the early shift monitoring traffic out by Miller's farm."

"That's in the boonies. There isn't another house for miles."

"Exactly."

Heather winced. "Is he still being punished for helping you with Jessica?"

Chris had given me valuable information when someone murdered my friend.

"He won't admit it, but probably."

Heather got up and disappeared into the kitchen for a few minutes while I packed up my tools. She came out with two coffees and a box of pastries. "A bribe."

"For what?" I blinked.

"For him to tell you about the case."

I laughed and accepted the gift. I shuffled out to my car with my toolbox under one arm, my purse under the other, and the coffees and boxed baked goods balanced between my hands.

The hair on the back of my neck stood up as I approached my vehicle. I set my stuff down on the curb and inched toward the car. I tried the handle and found the door unlocked. *Did I lock you?* I replayed the morning in my head, but everything pre-coffee was a blur. I took my time packing up my car. After each item, I searched around the trunk and seats.

Nothing had moved, but I felt with certainty, when I climbed into my car, that someone else had been there. I quickly searched the glove compartment and the center console. Everything was as I'd left it.

The hairs on the back of my neck would not go down. I hunched my shoulders and continued searching. I felt under the seat and groped around under the steering column. My fingers brushed against something small and round under the wheel.

Despite the tenseness in my body, my heart rate slowed as I touched it. A feeling of boredom washed over me, mixed with a tinge of skepticism. I worked my nails around the edge of the object and pulled it loose.

It was a small bug with a microphone in it.

I cursed under my breath. If only I'd found my gran's notebook the night before. I hadn't practiced the memory-recall spell often enough to remember the words. In my hands I had an object that could listen, yet I couldn't use my skills to tap into it and hear what it'd heard.

Wait. Why is someone bugging my car? My mind went to Jacob, but I dismissed him almost as quickly. If he worked for the IRS and they wanted to investigate me, they would have much more nondescript tech than this. It was obviously a bug. It had the look and feel of something available at an electronic spy store for amateurs. Someone else was spying on me.

I wrapped the bug in a napkin and shoved it into the trunk. If someone was spying on me, I didn't want to tip them off just yet that I knew, not until I could figure out who they were. They could listen to my trunk. Listening to hours of road noise would frustrate anyone.

The road all the way out by Miller's farm was empty. The twists and turns made it difficult to go much faster than twenty, but the last stretch was open road, and getting a lead foot was all too easy. I fought the urge. That would be ironic —getting pulled over for speeding on my way to see Chris, a deputy.

I pulled up next to his car and got out. He had a fifteen-minute break early in the morning, and we'd developed a routine to meet and share a cup of coffee. The parameters of our new relationship still weren't clear. So far, it involved weekly coffee and playful banter. We'd gone out to lunch once, but we had to cut it short. I was building up the confidence to ask him to dinner. The thought of it made my palms sweaty and my heart race out of control. Before my ex-husband, I'd only ever dated one other person. And I had never asked anyone out before. This was new territory.

I carried the drinks and baked goods over to him, and we sat down on the hood of his car. The wind bit into the skin of my hands, and we sipped our drinks in companionable silence.

"So what did I do to deserve pastries?" he asked, biting into a pumpkin Danish.

"Can't a girl just do something nice?"

He raised an eyebrow.

He shifted next to me, and my heart fluttered as his leg brushed mine. I ducked my head.

"I'm happy to spend time with you. With or without the added excuse of morning coffee. It's the second-best part of my week."

I scoffed. "Second-best?"

He nodded, a serious expression on his face. "We also closed a harrowing case. Princess Sparkle was lost for three days. It was touch-and-go for a bit, but we recovered her in the neighbor's kitchen. The roasted duck she was helping herself to was not so lucky."

I giggled and peeked at him through a curtain of my hair. He smiled at me. I brushed my hair behind my ear and met his gaze. "Well, I'm glad you rescued her from that ordeal."

"So, the baked goods?" He nibbled on the pumpkin Danish.

"They might also be an offering of sorts."

"An offering?" His smile widened into a grin.

"To butter you up."

He barked out a laugh. "For what?"

"For when I ask how the case is going."

He frowned and put the pastry down. "You know I can't talk to you about that."

I tracked his movements out of the corner of my eye. He sipped his coffee, his body tense next to me. *I could always make him relax.* I clenched my jaw. *No. If I want this to go somewhere, I can't use magic on him to change how he feels. That feels... wrong.*

He sighed and set the cup down. "Why do you care so much about this case? You didn't know the girl."

"I don't." I playfully poked him in the ribs with my elbow. "But your boss told me I can't get access to the home until you solve the case, and accessing the home is my job. And with all future assignments being held up until I wrap up this claim, I'm getting antsy."

"I've been working on calming him down, but he hasn't been happy with you ever since Theresa passed."

My jaw dropped. "Why? I had nothing to do with her death. She was in hospice. For cancer."

He cleared his throat and ran his fingers through his hair, which was getting long for him. His normally clean, clipped brown hair was a little shaggy around the edges. "I know that. But you have to understand. She had been fighting it for years. And he thinks when she found out, when you figured out what happened to their son... she gave up hope."

I blinked and slid back on the hood. *Hope that had been keeping her alive.* I opened and closed my mouth. *The sheriff thinks I took away her hope.*

"It doesn't help when you—"

My head jerked toward him. "Doesn't help when I what?"

He held his hands up. "Look, don't shoot the messenger."

I relaxed and placed my hand on his knee. It was warm and solid under my fingers. He covered my hand with his. My heart skipped a beat at the contact. I ducked my head, my hair sliding down to hide my face.

"It doesn't help when you're seen talking to the reporter, the one who broke the story." He squeezed my hand. "You really should let the professionals handle this. We know what we're doing."

"A professional? You do realize I've been investigating claims for well over fifteen years."

"A murder investigation isn't—"

"Are you still focused on Clint?"

"He is a person of interest."

I pulled my hand back. "Has no one stopped to ask how someone without a car could get from Oak Harbor to Point Pleasant in less than ten minutes?"

"What are you talking about?"

"Clint. How did he get from Oak Harbor to Point Pleasant in less than ten minutes?"

"He doesn't have an alibi."

"Of course he does. I called it in to your office days ago." I slid off the hood of the car and spun to face him, my hands on my hips. "Just because he didn't spend the night at Haven of Hope doesn't mean he didn't go there. He missed the curfew, so they couldn't let him in. So, tell me, how did he get from Oak Harbor to Point Pleasant?"

His jaw dropped, and he hopped down from the hood. He scrambled into his car and grabbed the walkie-talkie from the dash. "Peggy? Are you there?"

"You didn't know?" I stepped back.

He shook his head.

"Yes. What do you need?" Peggy's voice came out staticky.

"Could you ask Abbott to call the Haven of Hope and ask about Clint?" he asked, holding my gaze.

"Bob's already handled that."

"Could you ask him to do it anyway? Have him ask if Clint showed up past curfew the night of the fire." He gripped the walkie-talkie. He held his breath, waiting for a response.

The seconds dragged. I was holding my breath too.

"Fine. I'll ask him to do it when he comes in."

He dropped the walkie-talkie back down and took a step toward me. He raised his arms as if to pull me into a hug but swerved mid motion to run a hand through his hair.

I took a faltering step back. "But I called it in…"

"Who'd you talk to?"

"It was after hours. I left the message on your tip line."

He frowned. "Bob listens to those every morning."

"He ignored it because it came from me, didn't he?"

Chris opened his mouth to say something and stopped. He shrugged.

I took another step back. "I really should get back to town."

He frowned. "And I should get back to work. Break's over."

He watched me as I got into my car and drove away. I could feel his gaze following my vehicle until I entered the tree line. Someday, I would figure out if these were dates or not. *Or is this what it feels like to be friends with a very attractive guy? Will it wreck everything if I ask him out?*

CHAPTER 16

After coffee with Chris, I returned to my office to discover I'd received three claims from a contact I'd sent a gift basket to. I squealed and danced around the office. Fall weather brought wind and, with it, wind damage. I quickly responded to the assignments and set up the inspections for later in the day. I spent the rest of my morning running from inspection to inspection, clambering up ladders to test how brittle the shingles were and using my drone to take pictures of the roofs from all angles. Getting a quick turnaround would go a long way to proving my worth.

I worked through lunch. Halfway through my last inspection, my stomach started growling so loudly the client heard me. He kindly recommended a drive-through burger joint a few blocks away that stuffed cheese into the patty.

I sat in my car outside Seawall Park. I didn't make it into Langley very often, but it was a cute community. The burger was as delicious as it sounded, and I savored every bite. As I stared out at the water, the case invaded my thoughts. I stiffened. *Emily Gallagher. The boss's wife. She coaches a basketball team in Langley.* I pulled out my phone and searched for the community center website. The basketball team practiced three days a week, and today was one of them. While not at the top of my list, Emily was still a suspect, and a conversation without her husband there might be illuminating.

I drove straight to the community center. It was a squat industrial-style building with a domed roof. Every exterior surface was covered in murals painted by local artists. A weight settled onto my chest as I peered at it. The parking lot was half full. Mrs. Gallagher had been polite but hostile toward me during our first meeting. *How should I play this? Looking to volunteer? Finding a program for my daughter?* I slowed my breathing to calm myself and counted back from ten before getting out of the car.

The squeak of tennis shoes greeted me when I stepped inside. I scanned the area. The lobby was empty. I followed the sound of running to the gymnasium. Over a dozen men were running back and forth, warming up. They ranged in age from young teenagers to graying grandfathers. One of the young boys stopped near me and guzzled water from a bottle.

I stepped up to him, a polite smile on my face. "Excuse me."

He wiped his mouth. "Did you need something, ma'am?"

"I was looking for the coach."

He jogged in place and stretched his hands over his head. "She stepped outside to take a call. She'll be back before the drills are over."

I nodded. He darted back onto the court and sprinted away. I followed the wall to a door in the back and stepped outside.

The chill air blew past me and yanked the door out of my hand. I lunged for it and caught it before the door slammed shut. I zipped my coat up over my hoodie and squinted into the darkness. The time was only six, and the sun had set. The lights at the rear of the building were dim, leaving most of the small alleyway in deep shadow.

I inched forward until voices came to me on the wind, a half whispered, angry conversation. I peeked around the corner and froze.

Emily Gallagher was standing face-to-face with the mysterious man from the parking garage, Tina's stalker. The security guard was right. I recognized him immediately. They were standing a few feet from a streetlight. I had no way to get closer without them noticing.

I ducked out of sight and pressed myself against the building. *While I can't get closer, that doesn't mean I can't listen in.* Fortunately for me, I had practiced the heightened-senses spell frequently enough to remember the words. I gritted my teeth and whispered the words. At first, focusing past the stinging cold was hard, but I dampened the sensations I didn't need one by one until only hearing was left.

"When I said 'nothing interesting,' I meant it. You can listen to the tape yourself, but all she's been doing is driving around all day," the man said. He had a crisp New England accent.

"Are you sure? She was asking about Tina." Emily's words were half garbled by the wind snapping a twig on a tree.

"I'm running a background check. But so far, it's clean. She's a claims adjuster, probably doing her job. I can—"

The door next to me opened, and the squeak of sneakers thundered into my ears. I winced at the sudden loudness and dropped the spell.

A player ducked outside and yelled, "Coach! Drills are done!"

I retreated into the shadows and scampered along the wall to the far corner. I ducked around the corner as Emily arrived at the door.

Emily would be there a while, but the man she was talking to was probably on his way back to his car. He knew so much about me. I wanted to find out more about him before meeting him face-to-face. This might be the only opportunity for me to follow him and figure out who he was. I went from car to car, reading the license plates. I paused at the red Ford Explorer I'd seen at the community college. Next to it was a rental. I snapped a picture of both vehicles and ran back to my car.

My mind was reeling as I hurriedly moved my car between two large trucks to hide it from view. *Driving around all day. He's the one who bugged my car. But why?* I slouched in my car as the rental drove past. The mysterious man was behind the wheel. He didn't look in my direction. I exhaled and started my engine. I waited five seconds and followed.

I gripped the steering wheel. *What am I doing? I'm not a cop.* I'd followed people who knew I was there before, but I'd never tailed anyone. Keeping track of him without getting too close was hard. I kept my eyes on his vehicle as he wove in and out of traffic a few cars ahead.

He turned onto the main road. My eyes flicked between him and signs for Langley Road, which headed out of town. The light ahead of us changed to yellow. He hit the gas and sped through the intersection as the car in front of me put on their brakes. I slammed on my brakes and slid to a stop.

"Shoot!" I slammed my hands onto the steering wheel and leaned over to peer around the car in front of me. The mysterious man turned right onto a side street.

I drummed my fingers against the steering wheel, waiting for the light to turn green. When it did, I impatiently inched forward until the car in front of me cleared the intersection going left. Then I gunned it and sped through after the man.

I took a right onto the side street.

The road was empty. I drove slowly down the block until I hit the end of a cul-de-sac and turned around. Too many alleys and connecting streets led to that road. Figuring out which one he'd taken was impossible.

I drove around the neighborhood for another half an hour before giving up. His car was nowhere in sight. I returned to the community center, but the Ford explorer was also gone. I cursed under my breath and drummed my fingers on the steering wheel. At least I had a picture of their cars. When I got home, I could use it to cast a locator spell. I slowed my breathing. *There is still time to figure this out.*

Every light on the way home had turned red as I approached, making the drive agonizingly long. While Langley was normally only a few minutes from Point Pleasant, every second stretched and warped until I seemed to have been driving for hours by the time I pulled into my driveway. From the trunk, I grabbed my home-inspection kit, which had a stack of maps tucked into a side pocket, and dashed toward the front door. I took the front steps two at a time as I fumbled with my keys.

I froze with the key in the lock. Voices were coming from inside the living room. I pressed my ear to the door.

"No. I'm still not sleeping well," Grace said.

"There's a good sleep specialist in Spokane." The next voice echoed like he was standing in a tunnel.

My heart dropped. I pressed myself into the door to steady myself. *Ed.* I hadn't spoken to my ex-husband in months, not since I'd announced my intention to move across the state. He hadn't batted an eye at the divorce, but the move he had objected to. *Grace needs a mother who is going to be present. Don't do this to her.* His words stung. He probably blamed me for her dropping out of university.

"I'll think about it."

I stepped away from the front door and peered into the living room window. Grace lay sprawled on the floor with her laptop open in front of her. Ed's face filled the screen. He would want me to encourage her to go home. I didn't have time for that conversation. I had to do the locator spell right away if I wanted to track down the mystery man that night. I slunk around the wraparound porch to the back, and I let myself in through the daylight basement. I tiptoed through the house to my room to retrieve the journal I'd found in the attic.

Older homes had smaller bedrooms, which made them easier to heat. But that left them with very little floor space, even the master bedrooms. I held the maps up and sighed. The living room and dining room were both out of the question.

Slipping out of the bedroom, I sneaked down to the basement. Charlie greeted me on the stairs and chirped. I pressed a finger to my lips and shushed him. He cocked his head to one side but remained silent as he followed me through the house.

I slipped into the darkroom in the basement and closed the door. Charlie jumped into his cat bed on the counter. He circled it twice and slumped down to watch me as I unfolded the maps and spread them out over the work surface. He chirped at me.

"I'm trying an alternate version of the locator spell."

He lifted his head and chirped again.

"Thank you for your vote of confidence." I chuckled.

He slow blinked and lowered his head back down. He rested his chin on his front paws and watched me through hooded eyes.

Not having room for the big map, I started with a blown-out version of Western Washington. It showed everything from the Canadian border in the north to the Oregon border in the south and stopped at Yakima Valley in the east. It was bigger than I needed, but the other maps broke it down to too fine a detail, and I had to make sure he was still on the island.

I opened the journal to the locator spell and found a few versions of it. So far, I'd only practiced the glowing-path version, but alternatives existed. They all involved a sympathetic object, but some included finding it on a map or spying on its location through an obsidian mirror. I scrawled a note to myself to look into buying one. This was the second spell that worked best with obsidian mirrors. Since that wasn't currently an option, I opted to use a map instead.

On one side of the map, I set my phone with the picture of the mystery man's car, and on the other side, I put the journal. I shook out my arms and began.

Motes of light spilled out of my mouth as I spoke. They danced over the map until they settled over Whidbey Island. They came to rest on the northern half of the island. I smiled and flipped to the next page. The lights didn't move to the next map. I sighed and released the spell.

"All right, then. A spell per map. Let's go."

I cast the spell two more times until I'd narrowed it down to a specific block in Oak Harbor. A tremor ran through my body, every muscle quivering with exhaustion. I slumped into a chair and grabbed my phone to look it up. Using Google Street View, I found the block. It was a two-lane road with trees on one side, and on the other, on the corner next to an auto mechanic, was an Enterprise.

I hung my head.

Did he see me?

My back spasmed. I had been hunched over the table for the last twenty minutes, casting spells. I stretched, trying to release the knot.

Charlie tapped his paw on the map.

"I know, buddy, I know. I have one more car to find." I rummaged in my bag and pulled out a power bar to refuel.

For the next set of spells, I pulled up a stool. I perched on the edge of the seat as I cast the first spell. Once again, the lights settled over Whidbey Island, but this time, they clustered along the southern part of the island. Three more tries narrowed the location of Emily's car down to a stretch of waterfront homes near Bells Beach. By the end, I was on my third power bar.

Using Google Street View again, I zoomed in on a specific

house. I recognized the home. Biting my lip, I scrolled through Emily's social media profile and stopped at a picture of her on her front porch with a fishing pole in one hand and a beer in the other.

I dropped my phone and sighed. The mystery man had returned his car, and she was at home. I had missed my opportunity to find anything useful.

When I poked my head into the hall, Grace's voice echoed down to me from the living room. I retreated into the darkroom once more. If I went upstairs, I would have to talk to Ed. My mind grappled with what to do next. Ed and I had a clean divorce. We'd both fallen out of love with each other so long before that it felt like a relief to both of us. That didn't mean I was ready to catch up or admit I was interested in his best friend from high school. I glanced at my kit. Over the past few days, I'd taken a few photos of Grace and Charlie together. I reached for my camera. I had time to kill, and developing film was always cathartic.

CHAPTER 17

The morning came too soon the next day. One thing had led to another, and I was in the darkroom, developing film and printing pictures, until well after midnight. Long gone were the days when I could stay up until two in the morning and wake up bright eyed and bushy tailed at six. Blurry eyed, I added an extra scoop of coffee to the pot.

The extra caffeine helped invigorate me. After my second cup, I was buzzing with energy. I packed up my kit for the day, cleaned the kitchen, took out the trash, and reorganized the junk drawer. It was seven o'clock, and I had another forty minutes to kill before I had to head into the office for the day.

I retreated to the darkroom and recreated the setup I'd used the previous night: the sketch of the journal on one side, the journal from the attic on the other, and a map between. If I couldn't find it in the house, maybe I'd left it somewhere else, like the office.

The locator spell was becoming easier to use with each attempt. The words came more naturally. I would be halfway through the spell, and the lights would coalesce. By the last word, they gathered together in a smaller point than the night before. The light didn't hover over the entire southern portion of the island—it hung over Point Pleasant.

I flipped to a map of the town and started again. The lights settled over my home on the map. "Okay. So it's at the house?"

I jumped in place to build the energy back up. While magic wasn't physically active, using it drained me as quickly as running a marathon. My heart raced in my chest. I closed my eyes and exhaled slowly through my mouth, counting backward from ten in my head.

I picked the drawing back up from the table and held it in view as I whispered another locator spell, the original version, the lighted path. Lights gathered in the room, pulsating as they swirled around me. After the last word left my mouth, I held my breath as the lights swirled and formed into a path.

I slumped as the path took form. It led straight from me to the book in my hand.

The spell had failed again. I had to find the journal the old-fashioned way. The locator spell wasn't going to work. I texted Betty to let her know I was still searching. She'd been texting me daily, asking for updates since I told her it was missing. She wrote back seconds later, telling me to try, try again, but at least I'd found the second one—although I should be more careful with that one than I was with the first.

I grumbled. The last place I could remember having my gran's lost journal was my bedroom. Having ten minutes before the time I normally left, I charged upstairs and tore apart the closet and dug through each of the drawers. I was half under the bed when a door slammed downstairs. I jerked up, hitting my head on a wooden support beam.

"I'm headed out!" Grace yelled from the living room.

I scrambled out from under the bed. *I should ask her about the journal again.* I jogged to the top of the stairs. "Hey, sweetie—"

The front door closed.

I sprinted down the steps and swung the front door open. Grace was already reversing out of the driveway. I sighed and headed back into the house. The eight o'clock start time was one I'd set for myself. If I was a few minutes late, it wouldn't hurt anyone.

I crawled back under the bed and pulled out the last few items stowed away in the corners. In my search, I'd found two lost socks, a stray hair tie, six cat toys, and a tube of lipstick so coated in dust that it had probably rolled out of sight in the eighties.

I sat on the bed and started a mental checklist of all the places I still had to search. I faltered as I added Grace's room to the list.

I peeked into her room. Clothes were strewn across the floor. A half-eaten box of cookies lay open on the bed. I scrunched up my nose and stepped inside. I hadn't been in her room without her permission since she was a little girl. With my shoulders hunched, I crept through the room. A pile of clothes was half under the bed. I shoved it to the side and peered underneath. Random socks, a few of Charlie's toys, and an assortment of hair ties littered the floor. I shoved the clothes back into place and moved over to the dresser.

I was pawing my way through the second drawer when the front door closed. I hadn't made it all the way to the door when Grace burst into the room.

She slid to a stop and stared at me. "What are you doing in here?"

"I thought I left something in here."

"What?" She crossed her arms.

"Some of your gran's things. She had a journal—"

"I can't believe you. I told you I didn't have it. It isn't in here." She scowled. "When did you stop trusting me?"

"I haven't been able to find it in a few days. I thought... I don't know. That I might have dropped it?"

"Just get out." Grace stepped to the side and pointed at the door.

I hovered for a second.

"Get out!"

"I'm sorry, sweetie. I didn't mean anything." I retreated from the room.

She slammed the door in my face.

My phone dinged in my pocket—one new email. *She's going to hate me now. I hope she doesn't leave because of this.* Over the years, I'd learned the best thing to do with Grace when she was upset was to give her space. My search would have to wait. The journal had been missing for a few days already, and the world hadn't ended. I grabbed my things and headed out the door with Charlie in tow.

Parking along the main drag filled up early. Charlie pranced next to me as I walked the two blocks to my office. He was becoming a local celebrity. Abby stepped out of her bistro and gifted him with a piece of salmon as we trotted by.

Seated in the lobby of my office was Clint. He sat hunched in a chair, a ball cap clasped in his hands. He was clean-shaven, with cropped hair. The transformation was miraculous. He almost looked like a different man. Hovering over him was a young woman who had his eyes. She surged toward me when I stepped inside.

"You must be Dani. The nice lady next door said you would have a cat with you. He is gorgeous," she gushed.

My eyes flicked between her and Clint. His eyes had lit up the second he saw Charlie. My cat straightened to his full height and strutted into the room. He paused in front of

Clint and headbutted Clint's hand. A smile broke out across the old man's face.

"I am, and you are...?" I shook the woman's hand.

"Chloe. I'm Clint's daughter." She pumped my hand up and down. "Deputy Harris told us about the extra work you put in. We understand we have you to thank for helping clear my dad's name."

My eyes watered as a smile broke out on my face as well. The joy in the room was infectious. "I'm so glad to hear they released him. What are you guys going to do now?"

"Now that I've found him again, I'm going to take him home. He's agreed to get treatment at the VA." Chloe looked back at her dad. "I am never letting you out of my sight again, you hear?"

He ducked his head and nodded. "Thank you, ma'am."

Chloe gathered her father's backpack from the floor, and they walked out together, arm in arm, heads held high. My heart swelled as they climbed into a car and drove away. Liv poked her head out from her office and gave me a thumbs-up. She pointed at her headset and ducked back into her office.

I floated into my office and sank into my chair, unable to get the grin off my face. Charlie jumped into my lap and rubbed his head against my shoulder. "I know, buddy. We did so good."

I chatted with Charlie as I switched on my computer and checked my emails. He chirped back at me periodically as I read through my messages. The fire report from the local investigator had come in.

It was a little shorter than expected, only six pages long, with four photos taking up the bulk of it. I scrolled to the last page and read the conclusion. *An electric fire?* I scrolled back through the images he'd attached. Not a single shot was included of the tires piled in the living room.

I plugged my phone into the computer and downloaded

all my photos. While they downloaded, I read through the entire report. It was sparse. Overall, it was very disappointing and shoddy work. I flipped through my photos and lined them up with what was in the report. It was like the investigator had ignored half the evidence on scene and focused on one small area. He was probably right that an electric fire had started it, but he didn't address the tires or the melted metal around the plug—nothing.

I bit my lip. The problem with small-town fire departments was they didn't always have the resources for big investigations. *Did he ignore it due to lack of funds... or another reason?*

I leaned back, blinking at my screen. I shook my head and forwarded the email to the desk adjuster with a quick message attached. "Got the fire report in. I think the report is missing a few things and recommend getting an engineer out there to look. Want me to get that set up?"

I received a response a few minutes later with approval and a budget. I texted Chris to ask if I could do my inspection since the fire report had been released, then I called the fire station to schedule a joint inspection. The inspector wasn't in yet, so I left a message.

Satisfied, I sat back and stared at the screen. Things were finally moving along. They had released Clint. The fire report, albeit lackluster, was complete. It was only a matter of time before I could get in there and finalize my very first claim assignment.

The rest of the morning passed in a blur. I hadn't really gotten to sit down and work for a long time. I typed up all my notes and wrote up repair estimates for the roofs I'd inspected the day before. Within a few hours, they were complete and off to the insurance companies for approval.

I was eating leftover Thai at my desk when my phone chimed with a new message. I paused at the name. *Madison? What is she messaging me about?* She was one of Grace's high school friends.

> **MADISON:**
> I haven't talked to her much since the semester started. She started getting really reclusive. I haven't seen her in almost three weeks.

I blinked and scrolled up, letting out a breath. *She's responding to my message.* I'd almost forgotten about reaching out.

> **DANI:**
> That's probably because she's out visiting me on Whidbey Island. She said she needed to take a break.

> **MADISON:**
> Glad to hear she's taking time. She needed it.

> **DANI:**
> Did something happen? She seems so worn down.

> **MADISON:**
> Not that I know. But you had a question about presents. Are you still needing gift tips?

I chewed on my lip. *Did she know something, or was she looking for the inside scoop as well?* I sighed and responded yes.

> **MADISON:**
> The only thing that seemed to make her happy was listening to music. Maybe a nice set of Bluetooth headphones?

I dropped the phone back on my desk. My contacting-a-friend Hail Mary hadn't worked. They didn't know what was going on in her life. *Maybe I should call Ed.* I gritted my teeth. I didn't need to talk to him to connect with my daughter.

I left Charlie sleeping at the office to go Christmas shopping for Grace. Traffic moved slowly around the lunchtime foot traffic. Almost all of downtown was row upon row of two-story brownstones with stores at street level and apartments above. The incoming mayor had promised to help revitalize the town. While he wasn't officially in the seat yet, Steven Bishop's fingerprints could be seen all over downtown. A hopeful energy filled the air. Shop signs were being spruced up. Restaurants were unveiling updated menus. The entire community was leaning into the rustic island charm that had put Point Pleasant on the map in the first place.

The one and only drawback so far had been that the only electronics store in town was also retooling. They'd struggled over the years, competing with the big-box stores, and had slowly reduced their inventory over the years. Now, however, they were an electronics repair facility only, with a side hustle of painting unique case art. I headed out of town and drove up the coast to a miniature outdoor mall in Freeland, where the store sat in a small complex with a coffee bar.

I wandered through the aisles, browsing the wide assortment of electronic accessories. So many headphones were there to choose from. I picked up a headset with cat ears that lit up. I grinned as I flipped them over in my hand. They weren't exactly small, but Grace seemed to love cats since having met Charlie.

A shiver went down my spine, and the hairs along my arms stood on end. My head jerked up, and I spun in place. No one was there, but I recognized the feeling of being watched. I gripped the headset and marched down the aisle, pushing past a woman with beach-blond hair. I half sprinted at the end and ducked around the corner behind a large monitor display.

I slid to a stop and waited with my breath held. Five seconds later, Tina's stalker rounded the corner. I stepped out from behind the display into his path. "What do you want?"

He grinned at me and held his hands out at his sides. "You caught me."

"Why are you following me?"

"It's my job. Mind if I reach into my pocket?"

I squinted at him and nodded my head.

He made a show out of reaching into his inside pocket and pulled out a business card. He held it out for me. When I reached for it, he playfully pulled it back before relenting and letting me take it. I gritted my teeth as I turned it over in my hands. In a plain black script, it said Derrick Miller, Private Investigator. On the back was a phone number with a license number printed in the bottom left corner.

I raised an eyebrow. "Someone paid you to follow me?"

He shrugged. "And you live a thoroughly boring life. But since I can go back to my employer and confirm you are not, in fact, sleeping with her husband, I think my job here is done."

I blinked. *Sleeping with her husband? Did she kill Tina out of jealousy?* I cleared my throat. "Is that why you were following Tina?"

"I can neither confirm nor deny." He shrugged again.

"Look, you seem like a nice lady. Mind if I give you a piece of advice?"

I blinked at him. *This whole thing is bizarre.* "Okay."

"If you're going to follow someone, you really have to work on your tailing skills."

My jaw dropped, and I began spluttering excuses.

He chuckled. "Honestly, the only person I've seen who is worse than you is whoever has been following you around. For someone who leads such a boring life, I don't get why so many people want to keep tabs on you."

I froze. "Someone's been following me?"

He nodded.

"Who?"

He went to shrug again but stopped midmotion. He stepped in closer and held my gaze. "I'm sorry. They didn't pay me to check. But I recognize a tail when I see one."

He stepped awkwardly away and disappeared down the next aisle. I stood, headphones in hand, my mind reeling. He was a private eye, which solved one mystery and took him off the suspect list. But the exchange left me uneasy. I bought the headphones and drove back into town in a daze. Someone was following me. *Why?*

CHAPTER 18

My mind was spinning. I drove into town, gripping the steering wheel and checking my mirrors every few seconds. I focused on every car that stayed behind me for more than a block. That was exhausting, so I stopped by the Bizzy Bean on my way back into the office. Heather had a way of calming me down. As I stepped inside, I let out a low whistle. Since my last visit, she'd finished the enclosure. She had changed my design slightly, leaving a small bar section in front of the windows outside the plexiglass walls, and installed two sets of doors to get inside: one by the counter and one by the window bar. The cafe was brimming with customers, who bantered back and forth over what glass-painting theme Heather should go with the next month since she had so much more glass real estate.

"Wow. Heather. It looks so good," I said as I walked up to the counter.

Heather beamed. "It really came together well."

"When did you have time to do all this work?"

"I had to make the time. I got a notice that they were moving the health inspection up to today. Luckily, Chris was around and volunteered to lend a hand."

"How did the inspection go?"

"It's in twenty minutes." She grimaced.

"Sorry I couldn't help more. But it looks great. I'm sure they're going to be impressed."

"I hope so. And you helped a ton. I wouldn't have thought about building the enclosure if it wasn't for you." She walked around the counter and pulled me into a hug. "How's the case coming along? I couldn't get one word out of Chris about it."

I glowered at her. I didn't have much of an update. She led me to our favorite table in the back and squeezed my hand as we sat down. I told her the recent events. She gasped when I got to the part where Derrick had revealed someone was following me.

"I have no idea who he could be. All I can think is I must be onto something. Otherwise, why follow me, right?" I bit my lip.

"Are you thinking about backing off?"

I straightened my shoulders and gripped the edge of the table. "Never."

"I can't believe you're not more freaked out. Maybe I'll be freaked out for the both of us." She sighed. "So, what's next?"

"I honestly don't know. On the list are"—I ticked things off on my fingers—"talk to the ex-boyfriend, finish my interview with Owen, and figure out who the mystery man from the boat was. Part of me suspects it was Owen. But if it was, that doesn't concretely answer who did it. Both Owen and his wife are tall enough to be the person Willy saw leave her house the night of the fire. If it wasn't, then who else could it be?"

"Has the ex messaged you back?"

"Not yet." I slumped into the booth. "I also need to get into Tina's house to inspect it for damage. The fire report was a complete joke."

"He's new, right?"

I nodded and leaned out of the booth and waved over the Retirees. They tittered to each other as they shuffled en masse to the table.

"Have you ladies heard anything interesting about the new fire investigator?"

"Brad Parsons? The guy from Louisiana?" Agnes asked.

"That's the one."

After the Retirees exchanged a look, Betty stepped forward. "Word on the grapevine is they blacklisted him in Louisiana."

Sarah picked up where Betty left off. "He couldn't get work in the South, and his whole family had to uproot themselves and move out here."

Agnes leaned in and stage-whispered the next part. "It was all very hush-hush. No one local knows what happened. Some college connections put pressure on the local precinct to not ask those sorts of questions."

They hovered for a few more minutes to speculate before returning to their table. *Blacklisted? What did he do?*

"What are you thinking?" Heather slid forward on the bench.

I pulled out my laptop and got to work. "Research." I started with trying to find news articles from Louisiana's small-town papers. What I'd learned from the *Island County Gazette* was that local scandals frequented the pages of small-town papers but rarely made waves outside into statewide or national news.

Nothing exciting was listed in any of them. Every news article about him was him helping to solve a case or being awarded for exemplary service. The last news article described him being promoted to senior fire investigator by the area chief out of Baton Rouge. In a photo, he stood smiling next to an old grizzled man and the man's wife. I squinted at her. She seemed out of place, wearing a skintight red dress. Her blond hair was in a half updo with long strands hanging down on either side of her face. Everything about her was glamorous and played at being sophisticated, from her dress to her clutch and right down to the silver rose necklace around her throat.

Next, I checked to see if he was on LinkedIn. He was, and he had an impressive resume. He'd climbed through the ranks and had a very promising career. And then it took a hard left turn last year when he moved out here for a less senior title. I drummed my fingers on the desk. A step back like that could bruise the ego and make it hard to care. I scrolled down to the bottom where his education was listed, and I smiled.

"Did you find something?"

"Guess who's a member of his fraternity?"

Heather grinned as I flipped the screen around.

Owen Gallagher, Tina's boss.

The bell above the door chimed. Heather slid out to see who it was. She ducked her head back in. "It's the health inspector."

I raised my hands and crossed my fingers. "Good luck."

"Thanks." She straightened, smoothed down her shirt, and went to greet him. "You're right on time. Let me show you around."

My conversation with Heather energized me to keep pushing. One thing I'd learned after years in the field was that sometimes, the only way to get someone to talk to you was to make a cold call. I drove straight to the fire station to speak to the fire investigator. I was so focused on checking for a tail that I almost missed my turn.

Like most of Point Pleasant, the fire department was in a historic structure. The building sat perched on top of a hill overlooking the town. The sun was dipping below the horizon, and the sky was a brilliant purple. I pulled out my camera and took a photo of the skyline before the sun set.

I capped my camera and strode into the station. The entrance hall had exposed red brick and original maple hardwood floors. I wandered from room to room, searching for someone to talk to. I walked through a set of double doors, and the maple hardwood changed to a peeling vinyl. Fluorescent lights flickered overhead, giving off a steady electric buzz. A massive seventy-five-inch TV hung on the back wall, surrounded by beat-up couches and beanbag chairs.

A burly man was sleeping, sprawled out on one of the chairs. Next to him, typing away on her cell phone, was a broad-shouldered woman with tattoos running down both arms. She looked up as I entered the room.

"Can I help you?" She climbed over the back of the couch and strode toward me across the room. Her footfalls fell heavy, but the man slept through it.

"Is Mr. Parsons around? I wanted to get on his schedule."

"He should be around soon." She came to a stop in front of me and relaxed into a parade rest position. "Did you need to speak with him specifically, or is it something any firefighter might be able to assist you with?"

I fished my business card out of my purse and handed it over. "I'm handling the claim for the house fire on Vanguard. If he'll be back soon, I don't mind waiting."

"I'll show you to his office."

I followed her down a short hallway. The paint on most of the doors was peeling, but his door was fresh. She held the door open for me, and I took a seat.

She hovered in the doorway. "For his schedule, were you planning on meeting with him alone?"

I cocked my head to one side. "Maybe. Is that a problem?"

She glanced over her shoulder and lowered her voice. "He can get a little overly familiar with women sometimes."

I blinked and opened and closed my mouth. "Thank you."

147

She smiled and continued to hover in the doorway until footsteps echoed down the hall. She backed out and was replaced a moment later by Brad. He scowled when he saw me, but that quickly shifted to a warm smile that didn't quite reach his eyes. "Miss Williams, was it? To what do I owe this pleasure?"

I fidgeted in my seat. My eyes swept his desk and stopped at a picture of his wife. "Is that your wife?" I picked up the photo. "She's pretty."

He took a seat behind his desk. I stared at the photo. She was a petite beach blonde with a smattering of freckles across her face. Around her neck was a familiar necklace, a silver rose.

He reached for the picture. "Yes. The love of my life."

The words had that hollow sound people make when they're lying. *The wife of the fire chief. She wore the same necklace.* I handed the picture back and forced a smile to my face. *It's possible they go to the same jeweler, but I'm willing to bet money on it being a gift from him. Scandal found.*

"I got a copy of the fire report this morning. It didn't have everything I need, so I will have to get back on site to look around myself. I wanted to give you the courtesy of being there for the inspection."

His smile widened, and he spread his hands out, palms up in a mock shrug. "It hasn't been released yet. I can't put an insurance inspection on my schedule until the sheriff gives the go-ahead."

"If you can't inspect it with me, are you going to complete the report? It's a lot shorter than I was expecting. The tires weren't mentioned at all."

"The report is done. If there isn't anything else, I have a busy day ahead."

I stood. "Do you have my card?"

He nodded, still smiling.

"Call me when you're ready to schedule something. I

know I'll be in there the minute the site gets opened back up." I paused in the doorway. "Oh, and I think I bumped into an old college friend of yours."

He raised his eyebrows.

"Owen?" I asked.

A flash of recognition was quickly replaced with a bored expression. "Is there a point to this?"

I shrugged. "It's a small world. That's all. Have a nice day."

His eyes bored into my back as I walked away. Something about his stare was predatory. I mentally added him to the list of suspects. *But why? Did he know Tina?*

I sat in my car and stared up at the fire station, swallowing the bile that had formed at the back of my throat. My heart was pounding from my meeting with the fire investigator. I emailed Katie Cole at the financial aid office to set up another meeting with Owen. Gritting my teeth, I sent another text to Jacob, asking to meet him as well. I reread the message. It was too polite and easily ignored. I added, "It looks like they might rule the fire an accident. Do you believe it was? I don't."

CHAPTER 19

The shrill tones of my phone pierced my dreams. I squinted at my clock on the nightstand. The time was five thirty in the morning. I groped for the phone to silence it and froze when I saw the name, Jacob Bryant. I sat bolt upright in bed and answered it.

"I'm ready to talk."

"Okay. When—"

"I'm on the island and am boarding the ferry that leaves for Mukilteo a few minutes after six. If you want to know what I know, meet me now."

He hung up. I scrambled out of bed and threw a sweatshirt and pants on. I hopped around the room as I put on socks and shoved my feet into work boots. Two minutes later, I was running out the front door then speeding out of my driveway.

I parked at the first open spot I found and sprinted toward the waiting area. Jacob was standing under a streetlight, his hands shoved into his pockets and his shoulders hunched. I slowed my pace as I approached and tried to fix my hair. It was a mess, with flyaway hairs sticking out at all angles. I hadn't had time to brush it before I left. I put up my hood and stepped into the light next to him.

"You came." He shuffled his feet.

"You didn't give me much of an option." I only had one chance at this conversation and had to swing for the fences. "Jacob."

He flinched. "How much do you know?"

"Not everything. Not why."

"I was the only one who looked young enough to be a student. I had never done undercover work before. And it was supposed to be a simple first assignment, you know? I only had to work with our informant on campus."

My head spun. *Informant? Undercover? I don't know what I was expecting, but not that. Who does he work for? The IRS?* I pushed a smile onto my face. People always said more when they thought you were knowledgeable.

His hands trembled as he ran his fingers through his hair. He looked around, wide-eyed, his breath coming out in quick puffs of steam. "Everything was going great for the first few months. Tina delivered like clockwork."

"What was she bringing you?"

He blinked at me. "I can't say. Something spooked her, though. She tried to back out."

"What spooked her?" I inched in closer.

"I don't know." He shuddered as he tried to hold back a sob. "She wouldn't talk to me about it."

My heart broke watching him. He was like a scared deer. Any quick movements, and he might bolt. I couldn't move toward him to comfort him, so I shifted my tone instead. "You couldn't have known something would happen."

"But what if it's my fault? I tried to convince her to keep going. We were almost done building the case."

"Before this, did it seem like the investigation was going to put her in danger?"

"No. Owen…" He closed his eyes and swallowed. "Owen

didn't seem dangerous. He was just another white-collar criminal, embezzling money from his employer. But since it happened, I can't get it out of my head. Did he do something to her? Did he hurt her because of the position I put her in?"

"Did she come to you first, or did you guys find her?"

He wiped away a tear. "She came to us."

"Then it wasn't a position you put her in. She wanted to help."

He sniffed. "You're right. Gosh. I shouldn't be telling you any of this. I could lose my job."

I squeezed his shoulder. "I'll do what I can to keep this all between you and me."

He glanced behind him at the ferry. "I should get on this."

"Will I be able to talk to you again?"

"Probably not. I'm being transferred out East. There's no need for a handler without a confidential informant." He walked through the gates to board the ferry.

The streets were mostly empty that time of morning, heading into downtown. A pair of headlights appeared behind me about half a block after I left the dock area. After my run-in with the private investigator, I was on high alert. I took a random side street. The car followed.

I gripped the steering wheel and made another random turn, going deeper into town. My gaze flicked between the roadway and my rearview mirror. I held my breath. When I was half a block down, the same set of headlights followed me onto the street.

I fought the urge to pick up speed and continued toward downtown proper. I cursed as I turned onto Marine View Drive. They'd blocked the parking up and down the street for road work, and most of the parking on the side streets was already filling up. I drove past my office. The agency light was already on. Ever since having her baby, Olivia had a hard time sleeping in and frequently arrived early to get a jump start on her paperwork. I exhaled and drove back around the block.

The headlights followed each of my turns. I circled the block, scanning the side streets for the closest spot. The closest one was almost a block and a half away. My eyes flicked between the headlights in my rearview and the spot. *I can't drive around forever. Chris?* The road out to the sheriff's office had one too many blind spots. If the person following me wanted to hurt me, no one would be around to see it. At least here, I had someone close by.

My hands trembled as I pulled into the space and climbed out of my car. The hair stood up on the back of my neck as I strode down the sidewalk. I hugged my sweatshirt and glanced over my shoulder. The vehicle was inching down the road at the same pace I was walking. I squinted against the headlights. The car was too dark for me to make out its type, but it was big. I quickened my pace, and the car followed suit.

As I rounded the corner, I ran. The car gunned its engine and sped toward me. My heart raced in my chest as I surged forward. I glanced over my shoulder. The headlights were bright and directed almost straight at me.

I barreled into the doors of the agency. They slammed open. I stumbled through and slid to a stop on my hands and knees. I scrambled up and rushed to the door to close it. The vehicle sped past the door. I barely had time to register it was a red SUV before it disappeared down the block.

Olivia poked her head out of her office. "What was that?"

I stood there, trembling. I fumbled with the lock on the door. It clicked shut on my second attempt.

Olivia tentatively put a hand on my shoulder. I burst into tears. She pulled me into a hug, and I gripped her, sobbing into her shoulder.

"Someone followed me into town," I said. "I thought they were going to run me over."

She patted my hair as she held me. "We should call the sheriff."

I pulled back and wiped my face. "I don't know. What is he going to do?"

She pulled a tissue out of her pocket and shoved it into my hands. "Investigate."

"He isn't exactly my biggest fan."

"Well, fortunately for you"—she squeezed my hand—"he rarely responds to things in person. It'll probably be Chris or Harrison."

I blew my nose. "That doesn't sound too bad."

"Good. Because I'm calling them either way." She squeezed my hand again and led me into her office to sit and wait.

CHAPTER 20

Olivia sat with me until Chris and Harrison arrived. When Chris stepped into the room, my eyes were red rimmed, and I clutched at the remains of the tissue Olivia had given me. He froze in the doorway. Then, jaw clenched, he stepped into the room, letting Harrison in behind him. Harrison ducked through the doorway, bumping into a lamp next to the door. His long limbs flailed as he lunged to catch it before it hit the ground.

"Sorry," he grumbled.

A laugh bubbled out of me as he fought with the cord. The tension in Chris's shoulders eased at the sound.

"Abbott, why don't you do a quick pass of the neighborhood while I conduct the interview?"

Harrison nodded and backed out of the room.

Olivia stood and busied herself in the break room.

Chris sat down next to me, his eyes searching. "Are you okay?"

"I will be."

"Can you tell me what happened?" He pulled out a notebook.

I told him almost everything. The only part I left out was

155

the details of my conversation with Jacob. I'd promised not to tell anyone he was working undercover, so I left that vague and mentioned Tina's recent house painting instead.

"Did you see the driver?"

I shook my head. "But I know someone who drives a red Ford Explorer. Owen Gallagher. Tina's boss. I've been working on the claim, and I've been trying to schedule a meeting with him. I messaged his office last night about it. Have you looked into him for her murder?"

"We did." He frowned and crossed his arms. "He has an airtight alibi."

"What if—"

"He won tickets to a hockey game. It involved meeting the team. It was a full-day affair. There's video footage of him being with them all day and most of the night. He never left the arena."

I sat back. I'd been so sure it was him. "What about his wife?"

"I don't think she was there. The sheriff cleared her. As far as we can tell, Emily didn't know Tina." Chris squeezed my hand. He left his hand covering mine and rubbed his thumb against my wrist.

I chewed on my lip. She knew Tina—or at least of her. Emily's behavior didn't sit right, though. *Why keep working with a private investigator after the death? Unless she was trying to tie up loose ends?* "She—"

Harrison stepped back into the office and cleared his throat.

Chris leapt back and smoothed his pant leg. "Did you find something?"

"No." Harrison fidgeted with his hat. "I noticed a red-light camera down the block. I'll check it, but unless they ran it, it wouldn't pick anything up."

My eyes flicked between Harrison and Chris. *Is he embar-*

rassed to be seen touching me? I clenched my teeth and stood. "Thank you both for coming out."

Harrison nodded and backed out of the door. He waited in the lobby for his partner. Chris hovered next to me, a pained expression on his face. His hand hovered over my arm. "You'll be careful, won't you?"

I hunched my shoulders and pulled away from him. "You should get going. Your partner is waiting."

Part of me wanted him to stay, but we were in that unchartered territory between friends and more than friends. Or at least, I thought we were. His reaction to Harrison coming into the room was odd. At moments like this, I missed Ed. I missed having someone who would hold me. If Chris stayed and acted only as a friend, I didn't think I could handle it. If I couldn't have him hold me, then I preferred to be alone.

He squeezed my shoulder and stepped out into the lobby.

Olivia hovered around me for another twenty minutes before I could convince her she could get back to work. I retreated across the hall to my office and shut the blinds. The driver had to be Emily. No one else made sense. Time was of the essence. I had to find her if I wanted to prove she'd been following me. Although I hadn't tried the locator spell without a paper map before, I was willing to give it a shot. I pulled up Google Maps and the picture of Emily's car and cast the spell. I forced my will into it. *Please work. I need to know where her car is.*

Motes of light flitted around the room before settling over my monitor. I continued muttering the words of the spell. *Show me where her car is.* The light settled over Langley, only a few miles away. She could have gotten there easily enough. I zoomed in and cast the spell a second time. The motes of light settled over a parking lot downtown. I chewed on my lip. *She wouldn't do anything with witnesses. Even at this time of day, it'll be a crowded street.* I scribbled down the address, grabbed my bag, and headed out without a backward glance.

I drove straight to the parking lot and pulled in next to her vehicle. It was a paid lot. I prowled around her vehicle and peeked through the front window. A parking pass was sitting on the dashboard. I squinted at the fine print: "Printed at 6:30 a.m."

I sagged. The red SUV had been barreling toward me at the time. It couldn't have been her.

"What do you think you're doing?" Emily screeched.

I flinched away from her car and spun toward her.

"Oh, I should have known he was a bumbling idiot. You are, aren't you?" She loomed over me, tears forming at the corners of her eyes. "Are you sleeping with my husband too?"

"I'm not." I held up my hands and took a step back, bumping into her car. "Someone tried to run me off the road this morning... and I thought it was you."

She came up short. "What? Why?"

I rubbed my left arm. "Life's gotten a little weird lately."

She snorted. "So you're really not sleeping with Owen?"

"No. I just met him, and married-to-someone-else isn't my type."

"I wish married-to-someone-else wasn't anybody's type." She shuddered.

I peered over her shoulder. The building she'd come out of was a divorce attorney's office. All her rage made sense.

"Is that why you hired the private investigator?"

She cocked her eyebrow and snorted again. "So I was right—he wasn't any good."

"Oh, he was. I just... Like I said, life has been weird lately."

"I hired him after I found Owen's secret bank account he had been paying that girl's rent out of. We were so close to finding something, you know? Something to prove his infidelity. But now she's gone... and all I've got is bank statements. I hope it's enough."

"Where were you the night of the fire?"

She blinked. "With my team. We won our first game, so we were celebrating in Oak Harbor. Did you think I did it?"

Her words felt true. *I wonder if that's why the sheriff checked her off the list? She had an alibi.* "Life—"

"Has been weird lately," she finished for me.

I shrugged and stepped away from her car. She climbed inside and stared at me for a moment before driving away. The image of her lingered in my head for a long time—those sad eyes.

I mentally checked her name off the list.

Derrick didn't do it.

Jacob didn't do it.

Emily didn't do it.

Owen didn't do it. At least not himself.

Who did that leave? The mystery man from the boat. I didn't have any solid leads on who it could be. I needed to get into Tina's home and hope for a vision.

CHAPTER 21

I knew two ways to gain access to Tina's home—either through the sheriff or through the fire investigator, who had a big question mark in his past. *And a connection to Owen. An alibi doesn't mean innocent. He could have paid Brad to do it.* I grabbed one of the last remaining gift baskets from my office and took it with me to the fire station. I grinned. *Gain access to the site while getting a better read on a potential suspect. Two birds. One stone.* I repeated this phrase to myself as I parked and walked up to the precinct.

A group of firefighters stood gathered around a truck as I walked by. Brad wasn't with them, so I continued to his office.

I knocked on his door. No one answered, so I pushed it open and poked my head inside. The room was empty of people. I slipped inside and dropped the gift basket on a corner of his desk. My heart raced as I glanced down the hall. It was empty. *If I'm lucky, he's left something useful in his office.* I closed the door to his office and sat down next to his desk. I read through his calendar. It was sparse. The only investigation he'd gone out on personally was Tina's. The whole next week was empty. I tried the drawers at his desk. They were all locked.

As I pulled at a handle, the table wobbled, knocking the picture of his wife over. I picked it up and stared at it. The silver necklace drew my gaze. *I've seen you before.* I wracked my brain, trying to remember. The first thing that came to mind was the fire chief's wife from Louisiana, but that wasn't the only place I'd seen it.

Tina's video.

She'd been playing with a silver rose necklace identical to this one.

Footsteps echoed in the hall. I quickly snapped a picture of her photo. I scrambled to put it on the desk and get back to the gift basket. When the door swung open, I had the basket in hand.

"What are you doing in my office?" He stepped toward me. The glower that flashed on his face the first two times I met him wasn't replaced by a smile. It stayed in place, morphing into a scowl the longer he stared at me.

"I realized, last time I stopped by, that I forgot to bring my 'welcome to the neighborhood' gift basket." I smiled and held it up.

"That is unnecessary."

"I was hoping you might be willing to put me on your schedule for the joint Vanguard home inspection."

"No."

"Why? All the evidence—"

"Because I don't have to." He sneered at me.

"Didn't hurt to try." I flushed and stepped past him into the hall. "Have a nice day."

I scurried away. He followed me down the hall and to my car. He climbed into his work truck and drove behind me all the way into town. I gripped the steering wheel until my knuckles turned white. He wasn't hiding the fact he was following me. He rode my bumper. He was so close that his scowling face was reflected in my rearview mirror. I drove past the Bizzy Bean. Every space out front was filled with cars. Exactly like that morning, my heart was telling me I needed to end up somewhere with people.

As I was approaching Eats and Treats Bistro, a spot opened up right outside. I pulled in and dashed inside. I peered out the window. He had parked in the fire lane along the boardwalk right across the street and was standing, arms crossed, staring at the building.

What now, smarty pants?

Eats and Treats was a bistro run by Abby, a local culinary genius. Her place drew crowds from when it opened at nine until it closed at three to prepare for dinner. Every seat at the counter was claimed, and most of the booths along the walls were filled. I grabbed a table near the back of the restaurant.

I sat perched on the edge of my seat and watched the front door. A steady stream of customers came and went, but the fire investigator didn't come inside. I stood and peered back out the window. He stood next to his truck, arms crossed over his chest. I gritted my teeth and returned to my table. The delicious scent of bacon mixed with maple. My stomach grumbled. *If I'm going to be stuck here, I might as well make the most of it.*

The line at the counter wound around the room and came to a stop a few feet from where I was sitting. I joined the line. Fortunately, Abby ran a tight ship, so it moved quickly. I scanned the menu above the bright-red counter as I waited. It changed weekly. The specials that week were a butternut squash soup or a grilled pork chop with a persimmon sauce.

I couldn't decide by the time I got up there. I stared helplessly at the options while Abby smiled at me from behind the counter.

"Let me guess. Surprise you?" She grinned.

I nodded.

She handed me my order number, and I went back to my table. While I waited for my food, I made a list of all the things I knew. Over the past few days, I'd stowed a lot of papers in my purse. I pulled them out one by one and stacked them into piles by suspect. Owen's pile grew quickly with all his gambling receipts. I stared at the printouts I had of Jacob's real profile. They were useless. I'd just pulled the last piece of paper as my food arrived.

Abby had ordered me a sandwich and salad. I grinned as I took it all in. It was a turkey-and-prosciutto half sandwich. It was grilled, and smoked gouda dripped down the sides. The salad was unique. It had kumquats cut into thin slivers and pistachios. My mouth watered. I tore into it. After three bites, I forced myself to slow down so that I could savor every morsel. At the end of the meal, I pushed the plate away and leaned back into my chair, satisfied.

I re-sorted the papers. The only paper that didn't seem to belong was the guest-lecturer schedule from the school. Brad Parsons presented once a week at the college. I pulled up a copy of Tina's schedule, which I'd gotten from Katie. Her last class of the day let out at the exact same time. *Is he the man from the ferry? He's tall. Good looking. And if he took the ferry, they would have been on it at the same time every week.* I chewed on my lip and realized I was speculating. I wouldn't know for sure without asking Gwen.

I scrolled through all the photos and video I'd collected. I paused. Out of all the pictures I'd taken or downloaded, Tina wasn't in any of them. I hadn't gotten a copy of the video from the reporter. Other than my gut, I had nothing to show they knew each other or were connected. I gritted my teeth. *Then find it.*

Without a second thought, I dialed the reporter. She answered on the third ring.

"Was the necklace on her body?"

"The necklace?"

"The one she was wearing in the video. It was a silver rose."

Papers shuffled in the background. "I don't think so. Why?"

"Could you send me a copy of the video?" I held my breath.

"You're on to something, aren't you?"

"I have a hunch."

"Where are you?"

I fidgeted in my seat. "Eats and Treats."

"I know that place. I'll meet you there. We can exchange your hunch for my video in person."

"I'll see you soon."

I stood and peered outside. The chief was sitting in his vehicle, staring daggers at the door. *Chris, I wish you were here.* I gritted my teeth. *But I don't want to feel like our friendship embarrasses you twice in one day. I'm a big girl. I've got this. So long as I stay where there are people, I'll be safe.*

I returned to my table. My stomach was in knots. I sipped a cool glass of water to settle my nerves. More customers came and left while I waited. I peered inside my purse and fingered the edge of my gran's second journal, which I'd stowed inside. *It could have a way out of this predicament.* I flipped through the pages. Izzy plopped down across from me when I was halfway through the description of a basic glamor spell. I flinched and shoved the book back into my purse.

"So, what do you have?" she asked.

"Did you see who was parked across the street?" I asked.

She glanced over her shoulder. "The fire chief and his wife. Why are they here?"

I blinked and stood. I made my way to the window and peered outside. Brad leaned against the truck. Next to him stood his wife, her beach-blonde hair hanging in waves around her shoulders. She stood, perched on a pair of high heels. While petite, she wasn't a short woman to begin with. Her heels put her just over six feet. I chewed on my lip. *Beach-blonde hair... I've been seeing her all over town. Why was she following me? Did he kill Tina, and she's helping cover for him... or is it the other way around?*

I returned to my chair and slid the guest lecturer brochure across the table at the reporter. "It's all circumstantial. But I think they knew each other. He taught once a week at her school."

Her eyes flicked from the brochure to my face. "And this makes you think they are involved?"

I slid my phone across the table. The screen was open to a picture of Brad's wife. She squinted at it and zoomed in to get a better view of her necklace. Then I reached out for the phone and pulled up the photo from the Louisiana paper and handed it back.

"Who is she?"

"I think she's the reason he doesn't work in Louisiana anymore."

She sat back and stared at me. "And they are both wearing the same necklace as Tina."

I nodded.

"If there is something you can do with this"—she texted me the video—"then bring him down."

She stood and walked out of the restaurant, her head held high.

I shivered. Only one more thing to do—find Tina's necklace and connect it back to him. *Did they take it from her?* With them camped outside, I had no way to get out without thinking creatively. I packed my purse up and slipped into the bathroom.

The window was small and too high on the wall to escape through. I cracked it open to get some air. The stress of trying a new spell under pressure made the room seem muggy. I gulped in the fresh air and splashed water on my face.

"I've got this." I gripped the edge of the sink and stared at my reflection straight in the eye.

I pulled out the journal and flipped back to the glamor spell. This was the first spell that would affect people all around me. I steadied my breathing and started the words. Like my gran wrote repeatedly in her directions, my intention was everything. I needed an escape. I needed to get out of here unnoticed. And the only thing people didn't pay attention to around here were tourists.

The spell, if I understood it correctly, only worked for a few minutes at a time and took a lot of focus to maintain. It was a minor illusion spell that would make me look like someone else. I pictured a tourist in my mind. It was the end of the season, so the coats would be big and too puffy. I focused on the page as the light spilled out of my mouth and settled all over my body. When I lifted my gaze, my usual gray eyes had been replaced with brown. I smiled at the stranger's face in the mirror, shoved the journal back into the purse, and darted outside before the spell wore off.

Sweat beaded on my forehead as I walked down the block. Brad's wife stepped away from the pickup and stepped into my path. "Excuse me, ma'am."

I swallowed. I'd forgotten to include voice in my vision. The second I opened my mouth, I would sound like me. I smiled and stepped around her.

"I was wondering if you saw a woman inside." She smiled at me, a dimple forming in her cheek.

I coughed, forcing phlegm into my throat. When I spoke, my voice was as nasal as I could manage. "I wasn't paying much attention. I was looking for something spicy to clear my head cold." I inhaled deeply and held up a hand in mock anticipation of a sneeze.

She backed away from me, her nose scrunched up. "Never mind."

I pulled my hoodie up over my head. Out of the corner of my eye, the color of my hair was fluctuating from dirty blond to brown. I hunched my shoulders and shuffled away from them as quickly as I could without drawing too much attention. I gritted my teeth and focused on maintaining the magic. I forced myself to stroll in that rambling manner outsiders have. When I hit the end of the block, I darted around the corner and sprinted as the spell slipped from my grasp and faded. I ducked into an alley as the light over my skin pulsated.

I stared at my hands as my skin shifted from tanned to pale. I exhaled and slumped against the wall. The spell hadn't lasted long at all, but it worked. I was out. Now, I had to connect the dots. But where would the dots end? Brad or his wife?

CHAPTER 22

I called myself a cab and had it drop me off at a small family-owned rental car company. They were one of the few places I knew about that rented cars out by the hour. I picked a Volkswagen Jetta and purchased one of their customized area maps, which had tips and tricks for making the most out of a day trip to Whidbey Island. I grinned when I opened it and saw competing ads for Eats and Treats bistro and Abby's main rival for all the local cooking competitions, Willow's Slice of Life diner. Both had become local institutions over the past few years.

I drove around for half an hour, checking and rechecking my rearview mirror until I was certain no one had followed me. I pulled into a scenic lookout and parked between two large pine trees. They towered over the car and shielded me from onlookers.

Even with the seat pushed back as far as it would go, the map was too big to unfold all the way. I folded down the top of the map, which went all the way up to Deception Pass at the top of the island, and focused on Point Pleasant and the surrounding areas. I balanced the journal in my lap while I clasped the map and phone with the video in my hands.

Casting a locator spell from my car was much less comfortable than from the darkroom, but I didn't know for sure that they hadn't given up at the diner and decided to drive by my house instead. I couldn't risk them seeing the rental car and starting up the tail all over again.

By then, the spell was familiar, and the words came easily. Motes of light flowed directly from me to the map and settled over Tina's house. The necklace was still there. My hands trembled with excitement as I folded the map and set it aside.

Getting to Tina's took only five minutes. The scent of soot and ash had dissipated over the past few days. The recent rains had done a lot to mute the odor. I parked across the street from the house. Yellow caution tape flapped in the wind. It had come loose from where Harrison had pinned it.

I tried the locator spell a second time, using the first variant. A trail of light led from me into the house. I peered into the house. My heart wanted to follow the light, but my mind held me back. *Would the sheriff charge me with tampering with evidence if he found out I went into the crime scene? He's feeling vindictive.* I chewed on my lip. *He might even refer me to the Department of Insurance. I could lose my license.*

I kept one eye on the trail of light as I flipped through the journal to the glamor spell. I tried to hold the locator spell active as I whispered the words to the glamor spell, but focusing was hard. Motes of light flew around the car and pulsated wildly, becoming brighter and brighter by the second. I shielded my eyes and tried to drop both spells. The light didn't fade. I winced as the light flashed brightly in front of my face. I exhaled sharply and willed the magical effect to end.

The car was plunged into darkness, or at least what seemed like darkness after the brightness of the lights. I blinked, clearing my vision. The street was as it had been, quiet and damp. *No casting two spells at once. Noted.* I pinched the bridge of my nose and closed my eyes as I slumped into the seat. *Now what?* My head was spinning from my failed attempt. I fished a granola bar out of my purse and chewed it slowly until the pounding in my skull subsided.

If I couldn't hide, I would have to settle for knowing I wasn't being observed. I shook out my arms and closed my eyes. I whispered the words of the spell that would improve my senses. A dull ache in my shoulders throbbed as I became more in tune with my body. The stress of the day had settled into my upper back. I pushed that out of my mind and opened my eyes. The street was clear of all foot traffic. Half a block up, a family of small animals burrowed underground, the earth shifting around them. Willy was snoring inside his home. All the other houses stood silent, save for the gentle hum of electricity. A few blocks over, car tires crunched against the asphalt.

I dropped the spell to heighten my senses and began to recast the locator spell. While I was capable of casting a lot more spells than I could when I first started, my reserves were running low. That was it—I needed all my energy to get the spell to land.

The trail of light was weak. I got out of my car and stepped forward. The light began to fade. I gritted my teeth and pushed myself further. I held onto the magic with all my might as I scurried across the road and into Tina's home.

Rubble crunched underfoot. I barely had any time to take in my surroundings. The interior of the home had become a mess of soot and mud. Nothing had done anything to seal off the interior. Any other useful evidence there was probably long gone. I scrambled forward, following the trail to the necklace. I slipped on a sodden piece of debris and slid forward. As I caught myself on what remained of the kitchen wall, the light trail flickered. Cursing under my breath, I ran forward and chased it into the backyard. The trail ended at a tree, the light disappearing into the branches overhead. I glanced between the house and the tree and saw a clear line from the open bedroom window. *Did she throw it?* The trail of light flickered one last time and went out. *Is this why he was in the backyard on the first day after the fire?*

I walked around the tree, peering up into the branches. I couldn't see anything metallic from the ground. *It could be anywhere up there.* I gritted my teeth and started to climb. The uneven bark dug into my skin as I scaled the tree, climbing upward limb by limb. I paused every few feet, searching the nooks and crannies for a necklace. Halfway up the tree, the midday sun caught the edge of the silver rose caught in an old bird nest. I shimmied down the branch and snagged it with my fingertips. With the necklace in hand, I clambered back down the tree.

I paused on my way back to the car. *Is the necklace the only thing he was worried about? Is there something else I'm missing?* I spun in place, scanning the area. *Is there something else here?* I came to a stop, staring at a greenbelt across the street. Most of the trees were bare, but a few evergreens were mixed in, giving the space a vibrant appearance even this close to winter. The midday light glinted off an object halfway up a tree. I cocked my head to one side and ambled toward it.

Not until I was within a few feet could I make sense of what I was seeing. It was a camouflaged camera. The light had bounced off the lens, but everything else about the setup melted into the background. I glanced between the camera and the burned-out home. The angle was right.

I gritted my teeth. My gran's journal, the original journal she'd left me, had the perfect spell in it to figure out if this trail cam had seen anything. I should have practiced it more while I had the chance. Without the book, I couldn't experience the camera's memory.

I reached out to touch it. The only residual emotion attached to it was concentration mixed with hope. Based on the weathering around the strap, the trail cam had been there for a while.

I trudged my way through the underbrush toward Willy's house. A twig got caught on my pant leg. Shaking my leg, I kicked it loose and stumbled free onto his drive. I marched up to his door and knocked. Holding my breath, I listened for movement inside.

I knocked again, a little more loudly.

Footsteps pounded down the hall. Willy yanked the front door open, and he squinted out at me. "What?"

"I'm sorry, I just…" I faltered.

His expression softened. "Miss Williams, right? Are you still working on the fire claim?"

"I am." I jerked my head toward the green space. "I found a trail cam over there. Do you know who installed it?"

"I did. Had to get permission from the city parks to install it. Which was a bit of a rigmarole." He smiled, and the edges of his eyes crinkled. "My grandson loves raccoons. There's a family of them that live in a den in there. I compiled a video I sent him for his birthday. I'm working on another one for Christmas. This time, I'm going to give it to him in person."

"That's wonderful. I noticed the one in the tree points across the street."

He frowned. "Yeah. If only it could see that far. After the fire, I checked it, but nothing. If it had, I would have handed it over to the police in a heartbeat."

My heart sank. I'd found the necklace, but all the evidence I had found was circumstantial. I didn't have anything to definitively connect him to the murder. I murmured my thanks and trudged back to my car.

I was all out of ideas. I drove past the Bizzy Bean Cafe twice, my eyes on my rearview mirror, before heading in. Either

Brad and his wife were still back at Eats and Treats, or they'd given up for the day. I parked right out front and darted inside.

Heather was standing with the Retirees clustered around her as she opened a letter. They squealed and patted her on the back. Heather's eyes brimmed with tears. We locked eyes, and a grin broke out on her face. The group surged toward me. Before Heather could get a word out, the Retirees were talking over each other.

Betty pushed her way forward. "She got her A-plus rating back."

Sarah stepped around her and grabbed onto my arm. "They loved the enclosure. The inspector added a hand-written note!"

"They can't wait to see what type of window art she puts up," Agnes piped in. "Isn't it great? Not only her rating back, but she gained a new customer at the same time."

"That's wonderful," I half whispered.

"We should have a celebratory dinner. I wouldn't have been able to do it without you and Chris."

"That's wonderful," I repeated.

Heather batted the Retirees away. "Thank you, ladies. Your continued support means the world to me."

The Retirees tittered together for a few more minutes. Betty tried to catch my eye, but I averted my gaze. I hadn't found the journal. And while I was certain I was onto something, I couldn't prove it. I was a failure. I stood, half listening to their conversation. They'd quickly moved on to ideas for the next window display, starting an argument over whether it should be only Star on display or if it should include the foster kittens as well. Bickering, they stepped away and moved back to their table.

Heather held my gaze. "Everything okay?"

I shook my head. She glanced back over at the Retirees

and pulled me to the far table. I slid into the booth and stared at my hands.

"Tell me about it."

Though explaining my investigations was getting more and more difficult without touching on the witch stuff, I updated her as best I could. "Maybe if I tell Chris what I've found, he can find something to tie it all together. But I don't know. I think he might get away with it."

Heather pursed her lips and drummed her fingers on the table. "Even if he didn't miss anything, he thinks he did."

I inched forward until I was perched on the edge of my seat. "You're right."

"He doesn't know the trail cam didn't catch something."

"He doesn't. He's been so obvious about following me." I gripped the edge of the table and grinned as an idea formed in my head. "Which is kind of reckless." I leaned back and raised my voice, making sure it carried across the room. "I'm beyond frustrated. The sheriff hasn't cleared the scene." I nodded at Heather, encouraging her to follow my charade.

She raised her eyebrow. "What are they waiting for?"

"Who knows? But I can't wait for them anymore, so I'm moving forward with what I can. I found a trail cam pointed at the house. I've got a meeting with City Parks to pull it down in the morning."

The room had gotten quiet while we talked.

"What was that?" Heather whispered.

"The Retirees are here."

When I peeked over my shoulder, the Retirees were all sipping at their coffees and whispering to each other. They glanced at us with mischievous grins on their faces.

"The entire town will know by dinner."

Heather chuckled. "Now what?"

"Now, I need to catch him in the act and wheedle a confession out of him."

Heather frowned, shaking her head. "There you go again, putting yourself in danger."

"Don't worry. I'll be careful."

CHAPTER 23

For the rest of the evening, I couldn't relax. I spent the rest of the day trying to keep myself distracted. I sorted and rearranged the storage room and helped Grace move her furniture upstairs. After the sun went down, I checked my phone every twenty minutes before bouncing to the next activity. I deep cleaned the kitchen and darkroom and drew up a sketch of how I wanted to remodel the downstairs.

At sunset, I ducked out of the house, leaving Grace sprawled in her room, reading a book. I drove to Tina's house, checking my mirrors every few seconds as I approached her block. I didn't want to get too close, but I had to be close enough for the stakeout. My palms were sweaty. I drove past Tina's house and parked two blocks away. I shut off my engine and sat in the dark, watching the house.

Twenty minutes after I parked, a car pulled up behind me. I glanced in my mirrors as someone got out and walked toward my car. Heather crouched down at the passenger window and knocked. I unlocked the car, and she got in.

"What are you doing here?" I whispered, not sure why I

was whispering. Something about being on a stakeout was making me overly cautious.

"Making sure you stay safe," she whispered back. "And I brought snacks."

I squinted at her. After what had happened with Jessica, I could understand. Her killer had almost taken me out too.

"I figured if he takes a while, we can take turns. You might need to go to the bathroom, after all." She crossed her arms and stuck her nose in the air.

"Fine. But only because you brought snacks." I held my hand out for a cupcake she deposited into my palm.

We huddled together in the car as the minutes ticked by. A little past two o'clock, a car without its lights on pulled up next to the green space. I pressed myself against the edge of the steering wheel, careful not to hit the horn, and peered into the darkness. My eyes strained to make out the shape. Whoever it was was tall and broad. The dark shape climbed out of the car and crept toward the greenbelt.

"Is it him?" Heather whispered.

"I can't tell. I have to get closer."

I slipped out of my car and scurried toward them, walking low to hide behind the cars lining the street. I peered behind myself. Heather sat in the car, her phone clutched in her hand as she watched me prowl toward the figure in the dark.

I darted from one parked car to another, scampering quickly between the openings to avoid being seen. I came to a stop next to their truck. It was the fire investigator's vehicle. I crawled to the end of the cargo bed and peered past the tow hitch. Brad stood, almost hidden between the trees, searching for the trail cam. I fumbled with my phone. The night was much too dark for me to get a picture, especially from that distance. A picture wouldn't prove anything, though. I needed a confession. I opened my phone's recorder, slipped it back into my pocket, and stepped out from behind his truck.

"Is this what you were looking for?" I held up the silver necklace.

He spun and scowled at me. Any feigned politeness was gone from his face. His eyes bulged, and a vein in his forehead throbbed.

"I couldn't figure out why you were in the backyard. There wasn't any damage back there. But you were trying to find this."

He strode toward me. "That stupid cow threw it out the window."

"Is that why you killed her?" I took a faltering step back.

"No." He peered up and down the street. Heather wasn't in the car anymore. "She threatened me." He lunged toward me.

I darted out of his grasp and stumbled away from him. I swallowed. "A small girl like her?"

He prowled toward me, herding me toward the house. I backed up and tripped over the curb, falling into Tina's front yard. He grabbed the caution tape and yanked it loose. He wound it between his hands as he stalked toward me. "She deserved what she got. Just like you."

I darted away from him and ran through the burnt-out house. He chased after me. I bolted for the back door. I yanked on the handle, but the wood had swollen, and it refused to budge. He grabbed me from behind and pulled me backward. I threw my head into his face, slamming my skull into his nose. His grip loosened, and I slipped out of his grasp. I shoved him hard, and he fell backward. I ran as he cursed behind me.

He was much faster than me. I scrambled forward, searching wildly for a place to escape or hide. Large pieces of debris were scattered around the wreckage. I ducked behind the closest piece as he got back to his feet.

"You're not getting away from me," he growled.

I huddled behind the burned-out washing machine, hugging my knees. My reserves were running low. All the magic I'd cast over the past few days had really taken it out of me. All I had were the fumes left in the tank from the cupcake I'd eaten earlier. Shaking, I closed my eyes and tried to picture the pages of the journal as a siren wailed in the distance. *Please. Think of something useful. Stall until help arrives.*

My mind kept going back to the glamor spell. In my frazzled state, that was the only spell I could remember. I steadied myself as he prowled closer. The sirens stopped, and my heart plummeted. *Did Heather not call for help? Where is she?* Floorboards creaked as he made his way around the house, searching for me. I gritted my teeth and clenched my fists. She wouldn't have left me. *Help is coming.*

I pictured Tina and whispered the words to the spell. My skin warmed as the motes of light settled around me. The last flecks of light settled into my skin as he rounded the corner. He threw himself at me.

The moonlight caught my face as he shoved me down, and he froze. Confusion followed by terror filled his face. "Impossible." He scrambled back from me. "You're dead."

"Why did you kill Tina?" I stood.

"You were going to ruin everything," he cried and crawled backward away from me.

A bright light filled the space. Stunned, I dropped the spell and shielded my face.

"We have the place surrounded. Come out with your hands up."

Relief flooded through me at the sound of Chris's voice.

I fell to my knees as my adrenaline left me.

Brad stared at me, wide-eyed. "What are you?" he whispered.

I slumped against the pile of debris and stared at him as

he crawled backward away from me. He stood and walked out into the yard, his hands raised above his head. A small smile formed on my lips as Chris and Harrison surrounded him. They carted him away, his arms handcuffed behind his back.

Heather ran through the yard. She paused for a moment, her eyes searching my face, before throwing her arms around my neck. "I was so worried."

"I'm okay." I slumped against her, my eyes never leaving his face. "We got him."

He sat, covered in dirt and ash, as Bob read him his rights. We stood there watching until they drove away. The sheriff made Chris take him in, and he left Harrison behind to question me.

Heather did most of the talking. She'd found a blanket somewhere and had draped it over my shoulders. She shoved a thermos into my hands as she explained how we'd been up late, baking cookies. We ran out of butter, so we were driving around, trying to find some, when we saw Brad snooping around the burnt house. The ridiculous story rolled off her tongue. I coughed, trying to hide a laugh. Harrison didn't exactly buy the tale, but he let us go anyway.

She followed me home to make sure I got home all right. I shuffled into the house. Exhaustion filled me. I crawled into bed, covered in dirt. The sheets could be washed in the morning.

CHAPTER 24

With Grace in tow, I met Chris and Heather at Slice of Life a week later. Heather had insisted on treating us to dinner after all the help we'd provided to build the enclosure. I half suspected that was a way to get Chris and me to sit down together again. Our coffee date had been put on hold as he dealt with paperwork. He'd called once after the arrest, but I let it go to voicemail. The only call I'd returned was to Izzy. She was relieved to finally have answers and told me she owed me one.

After my ordeal with Jessica's killer, Chris had been there for me. Ever since, we'd been stuck in a weird limbo. With how he'd been behaving throughout the entire case, his career was clearly more important. The idea of asking for more—when he might not have been willing or able to give it —made my palms sweat and my heart race.

I paused at the entrance to the diner. Chris was sitting alone in the booth, and Heather hadn't arrived yet. Willow greeted me, and Chris twisted around in his seat to wave me over. I shuffled across the room and slid into the booth across from him. Grace plopped down next to me, her eyes wide as she took in all the art on the walls. We were in the section that had photos of the town from the 1950s all over the walls. They'd decorated the booth to match.

"I've got good news for you," Chris said. "We have officially released the scene."

The corner of my mouth quivered.

"It's official. Brad Parsons has confessed to everything." He chuckled and fidgeted with his napkin. "Including his attack on you."

I bowed my head.

He reached toward me but froze with his hand halfway across the table. My gaze flicked between him and Grace. She was staring at his hand. He withdrew it and cleared his throat. *He really doesn't know what he wants, does he?*

"Did you ever figure out who owned the red Ford Explorer?" I asked.

"Brad."

I frowned. "I thought he owned a truck."

"He does. He has two cars. One provided by the state, which is what he drove to work. And his SUV. Which his wife normally drives."

"And what about the tires?"

"How'd you know about the tires?" He gave a sheepish grin. "Never mind. You probably saw them the first day. Tina had a set of spare snow tires in her garage. He thought if the fire burned long and hot enough, we wouldn't be able to tell she was murdered. Since he was in charge of the fire investigation, he took them away before anyone could catalog them as evidence. Since all the postfire photos were his, we didn't know there had been tires on the scene until he told us."

"Did he say why he did it?" Grace asked.

"They were having an affair. She thought he was going to leave his wife. When she found out he wasn't, things got heated."

"No, I mean… Why did he attack my mom?"

"She confronted him at the scene."

"I meant before that. With the car."

He cleared his throat. "We are still working on that one. He tried to claim it was him, but he has an alibi for that date and time. We suspect it was probably his wife. She is being held and is facing accessory-to-murder charges."

"So my mom was just a loose end?" Grace's jaw jutted forward.

"Basically. Yeah." He squirmed in the seat as we both stared at him.

Heather slid into the booth next to Chris. "I hope you weren't waiting long."

"Nope," Chris said as I shook my head.

With Heather's arrival, we turned the conversation to more celebratory things. Heather had her A-plus rating back and was fully committed to making the cat cafe work. She'd reached out to all the area vets and local rescues and was going to partner with them to get cats adopted out to their "furever" homes. She brimmed with enthusiasm as she described her plans.

"And I was thinking about having a daily special where half the profits from the daily special would go to supporting cats at other shelters. What do you think?"

"That sounds wonderful," I said.

At the end of dinner, we shuffled outside, our bellies full and laughter on our lips. Heather had a way of bringing out the best in people. I couldn't stay bottled up when she was around. She pulled each of us into a hug and walked home. Grace slipped into the car to wait while Chris and I said our farewells. He hovered next to my car and fidgeted with his keys.

"I know we've tried grabbing a bite to eat together before. But I want to try again. And not just lunch this time but dinner." He was babbling.

I chewed on my lip. Dinner sounded wonderful, but he'd been a little hot and cold lately. It was hard to tell where his head was at. "Are you sure? I wouldn't want to embarrass you in front of your co-workers."

He flinched. "I'm sorry." He grabbed my hand and squeezed. "The sheriff has been breathing down my neck since Theresa passed. I thought if I created some distance, it would get better. But… it wasn't worth it. I would prefer getting frozen out of cases by the sheriff to giving you up."

I blushed and squeezed his hand back. "Dinner sounds wonderful."

I climbed into the car before I became a blathering idiot. Chris had a way of making my heart race. I couldn't stay mad at him, either. I grinned as I pulled away from the curb.

Grace rested her head against the window as I drove, her eyes closed.

"Did you enjoy the food?" I asked.

She nodded and pushed herself up. "We need to talk."

My heart plummeted. I flashed to my flirty farewell with Chris. "Nothing has happened. Although—"

Grace held up the lost journal. "Why didn't you tell me?"

My jaw dropped. I slammed on the brakes and pulled over to the side of the road, gripping the steering wheel. The hurt in her voice made my heart ache. I couldn't face her, so I stared straight ahead.

"Didn't I deserve to know? I'm your daughter."

"I'm sorry. It's new to me. I'm still trying to figure it all out."

"Is it supposed to hurt so much?" her voice cracked.

I spun in my seat and stared at her. Her words echoed in my head, mixing with the words of my gran's letter. The Sight could be too much to bear. It could drive you mad. It could be painful—deadly, even. *Did I do what Gran did? I kept it from her.* Tears pricked at the corners of my eyes. *Stupid. Haven't I learned anything about keeping family secrets?*

"Why does it hurt so much?" she sobbed.

"Are you… Are you a witch too?"

"I think so. I tried a few of these spells, and they worked. When I found it, I didn't believe it at first. I hoped there would be something in here to help with the dreams."

My hands trembled as I reached out for her, and I held her hands in mine.

"The nightmares won't stop. Every night. Every time I close my eyes, I can't stop seeing that woman."

"That woman?" I whispered. *I did this. I made her go through this alone.*

"She's screaming." She wiped at her face. "How did you find out? Did you recently get your powers too?"

"Yes. No? It's complicated. Mine came in when I was much younger. But my gran cast a spell to suppress them. I didn't know I had them until recently."

She squeezed my hand. "Can you suppress mine too? I just want to sleep."

"I don't know how she did it." I brushed her hair back behind her ears. "But I know someone who might. Are you sure that's what you want?"

"I don't know. Maybe? Yes. I need time to process all of this, and I can't do that without sleep."

My gaze didn't leave Grace's face as I called Betty.

"Have you found the book yet?" Betty asked as she picked up the phone.

"In a fashion." I slowly exhaled to steady my breathing. "I need your help. With Grace."

"What type of help?"

"I need to help her the way my gran helped me."

"Are you—"

"Not forever. She wants it. She needs some time to figure things out, and she can't, with how our family's gift works."

"It's very complicated. You're not ready for a spell like that."

"Please." I gripped the phone.

Betty became quiet. The seconds dragged on. I held my breath, waiting for her to speak.

"I'll ask Agnes."

I blinked. *Betty and Agnes? Is Sarah a witch too? Betty had said Gran was part of her coven. I hadn't thought to ask if there were any other members.*

I glanced up at Grace and forced a smile onto my face. "We're going to get through this."

She squeezed my hand again. "Together."

Did you miss seeing how Dani and Chris's first attempt at a date went? Interested in receiving bonus content? If so, join our mailing list and receive 'Foresight and the Fateful Ferry,' by scanning the QR code below.

Go on an adventure with Dani and Chris as they journey into Seattle for a fun day out, and things take a dramatic turn when they stumble upon a dead body on the ferry.

THE NEXT BOOK IN THE SERIES

Ready for the next enchanting adventure? Book 3, 'Divinations and the Disappearing Dead,' can be found by scanning the QR code below.

In book 3, as the holiday season approaches, the newly elected mayor starts a new tradition: A Winter Intern Extravaganza. Things take a dark turn when Dani Williams stumbles upon a lifeless body the morning after the kick-off party. To complicate matters, her visions foretell the death of Victor, the town's beloved medical examiner. Convinced these events are connected, Dani dives into another murder investigation.

Her personal life continues to become more complicated. Her daughter, Grace, is still struggling with nightmares and the Retirees aren't sure they can help. Meanwhile, a strain forms in her friendship with Heather, who remains oblivious to Dani's secret life as a witch. As tensions rise, bodies vanish, leaving Dani torn between preserving friendships and solving the mystery. Will she uncover the truth before her visions of Victor's death become a chilling reality?

Join Dani Williams on a magical journey through murder, self-discovery, and the complexities of friendship in this captivating paranormal cozy mystery.

ABOUT THE AUTHOR

Eloise Everhart lives in the Pacific Northwest. Her childhood was marked by voracious reading and tabletop roleplaying games, fueling her lifelong passion for storytelling.

By day, she's a dedicated insurance adjuster. It's a career that has honed her sharp eye for detail and developed her inquisitive mind—a skillset she now seamlessly integrates into her cozy mystery writing.

Beyond her storytelling ardor, Eloise is a devoted wife, sharing her home with a menagerie of rescued cats and dogs who have found their furever home in the Everhart household.

ACKNOWLEDGMENTS

In the process of writing this novel, I learned that the second book is just as difficult as the first. Once again, I have been fortunate to be supported by friends, family, and my wonderful editors. Without their contributions, this book would still be a mess on my hard drive.

To my editors Alyssa Hall and Kelly Reed, you added depth to my story, while helping me cut out the extraneous words that still litter my first drafts.

To my beloved husband, Nate, I will never understand how I got to be so lucky to have you in my life. You support me no matter what. Without you, my courage would waver, and I would become lost in the rewrites. To my sister, Andrea, I appreciate your eagle eyes going over the draft one last time, catching small things missed during the proof-reading process. It is a tidier book thanks to you. To my father, Chas, and my mother, Tammy, your continued words of encouragement give me strength. I will forever be grateful for your love and support.

As always, I would like to give a special thanks to someone who is no longer with us, Andrew Henderson. For years you were my writing partner, my confidant, and my greatest friend. You inspired me when I needed it most. Though we no longer tread the same path, I carry your memory with me always.

"Come on a journey with me."